WHILE
I WAS
GONE

Short Horrors
By
Andrew Cull.

Published by Vermillion2One Press 2025.

Cover design and artwork by
Michael Ramstead
www.michaelramstead.com

Copy editing by
Noel Osualdini.

ISBN: 978-0-6487315-8-0

Special thanks to:

Kerrie and Team Boo
Noel Osualdini
BP Gregory

WHILE I WAS GONE

Andrew Cull

Thanks so much for picking up this collection. I hope you dig the monsters I've captured within it. I wouldn't let them out, though, they're inclined to raise hell. Literally. The stories included here were written (mostly) during a particularly difficult time in my life: the two years I was being treated for cancer.

A content warning for this introduction: while I won't be going into detail about the symptoms of my illness[1], I feel it's appropriate to warn you that I will be covering bladder cancer, death and immunotherapy treatments.

In January 2023, I was diagnosed with a 4cm tumor in my bladder. The news came completely out of left field

---

[1] I've talked at length on Twitter about my symptoms and my journey to discovering that I had cancer. While I don't use Twitter anymore, I've left those posts up for reference. If you find yourself in a similar situation, my DMs are always open and I'm happy to help in any way I can. You should always consult a medical professional first, though.

for me. My symptoms had been mild, and I could easily have ignored them. I got the call with my diagnosis on the day our daughter started 4-year-old kindergarten. That was a day of complicated emotions.

I think that many cancer patients will tell you that the waiting is the worst part. The effects of treatment are bad but for me, nothing was as bad as the uncertainty that cancer brings with it. Once I'd been diagnosed, there was the wait for surgery, then the wait for a biopsy of the tumor so the cancer could be graded, then the wait for a second surgery, then the wait for my immunotherapy to start. Each of these pauses in the treatment left me mentally spinning. I tried to work, but couldn't spend more than a few minutes in front of my laptop. I was fidgety, angry, and often scared.

It wasn't long before I realized that most of the projects I had planned for 2023 would have to be delayed, or abandoned altogether, while I worked through my treatment. In May '23 we received the news that my tumor was a high-grade cancer. I was at kindergarten picking up our four-year-old when the call came through.

I was scheduled for further biopsies which would determine if I needed to have major surgery and, potentially, my whole bladder removed. It was a mentally raw time and probably the lowest point of my treatment.

Somehow, during all this, I managed to write "Carly's Wish" (huge thanks to John F. D. Taff and Shane Keene for their patience) and "The Scream" (again, thank you to Brandon Applegate for being so cool and patient with me).

Heading into the second surgery, the surgeon told me, "If you wake up with a catheter, we had to remove more cancer. If not, we only had to do biopsies and there weren't any signs that the cancer had spread."

I woke up without a catheter. The relief was huge. Although I had to wait for confirmation from the biopsies, it seemed that the first surgery had been a success. The cancer hadn't metastasized.

Here in Australia it takes a month for biopsy results to be returned. I got a call in June. The samples were negative. The doctor told me that I'd be referred for a six-week intensive course of BCG immunotherapy but that the results were the best possible outcome from the treatment so far.

We had a bit of a celebration that evening.

The next stage of my treatment involved six weeks of immunotherapy. Each Friday, I travelled to the Peter MacCallum Centre here in Melbourne for a dose of BCG.

That evening, the side effects of the treatment would kick in and they'd last for most of the weekend. By the Tuesday, I'd generally be back to myself, ready to do it all over again on the Friday.

I was lucky. The side effects for me mostly consisted of fatigue, muscle pain, cramps and nausea. I know that other patients receiving immunotherapy had to contend with symptoms much worse.

My body responded well to the BCG treatment, and after six weeks, further tests showed no signs of the cancer returning. I got a break in my treatment and was told it'd resume with monthly treatments for thirteen more sessions later in the year.

It was a marathon. All cancer treatment is a marathon. The initial surgery that'd seemed like such a big event was only a small part of eighteen months of cancer treatment and recovery.

I've said this lots of times: I was lucky. Yes, I had cancer. Yes, it was a particularly nasty type. But I was treated by a fantastic family doctor who went out of their way to help me through the initial stages of my diagnosis; I was referred to the Peter MacCallum Cancer Centre, where I received excellent care for almost two years (it's ongoing) and without having to pay anything for that care. Our treatments are covered by the public health system here in Australia.

I was lucky, but from my time on the cancer ward I know that others aren't. Cancer, while becoming more treatable, is still a terrifying diagnosis, and with good cause. Around the time of my final dose of BCG, my uncle passed away from the same type of cancer I was being treated for. That was a jarring reminder of how fortunate I'd been.

I'd gone to see a doctor at the first sign that something was wrong. I was initially brushed off and told I was too young to worry about cancer. I know they were trying to be reassuring, but the cancer clearly wasn't listening to them. A week later, my symptoms had recurred and I booked another appointment, this time with our family doctor. After that my diagnosis began in earnest.

If you think you're sick, see a medical professional. Early diagnosis is key to the successful treatment of cancer. Once it's spread, it's much harder to treat. I read a lot about cancer when I got my diagnosis; some of that material was helpful, some less so. It's easier, when you don't have such a frightening diagnosis hanging over you, to discern which is the best information and advice to take. But when you're looking down the barrel, so to speak, it's absolutely understandable that people go looking for miracles. Sadly, there are no miracle cures.

There are, however lots of people with their hand out on social media who'll promise you one for a fee.

I'm not going to lecture, but put your health in the hands of professionals. Read all you want outside of that, but don't delay your treatment, or worse, avoid having it because you've read of an unproven alternative. Discuss that alternative with your doctor. They'll happily answer your questions. If there were overnight cures for cancer, that's what you'd be receiving from a healthcare professional. Read, and read widely, but take that discussion to your doctor and involve them.

As I write this, I'm a month away from the next series of tests in my follow-up/maintenance treatment. I'll be visiting the hospital three times in May. Each time, I plan to leave a signed book in one of the patient free libraries at Peter Mac. So far, I've left sixteen over the past two years.

To be considered cancer free, I need to go five years without any recurrence of my cancer. I've got three more years to go, but I'm starting to look forward again. Cancer has a way of freezing you in the moment in the worst possible way. I'm getting back to writing. "The Gorey Man" was written this March. I'm slowly getting back to myself. Releasing this book was a big part of that. I know that a lot of you cheered me on while I was receiving my treatment and I can't thank you enough for that. It made a BIG difference. Y'all rock. Thank you!

A lot happened while I was gone but I'm very glad to be back.

Be cool. Be kind. Read horror books.

Andy Cull.
Melbourne, Australia.
April 2025.

CONTENTS

"CARLY'S WISH"

"The closer to the truth the lie is, the more likely they'll buy it. Understand?" Eddie, to his younger brother, summer 1985.

8th MAY 2022. 2100hrs P.S.T.

Travis Tanner: You're listening to the Crime Time podcast with myself, Travis Tanner, and my good friend and retired police detective, Bob Erskine. We've been talking to our guest, a man often known simply as 'Carly's dad,' David Scott. David, thanks for being with us tonight. We're going to go to the phones soon. But first, let's return to your new book for a moment.

David Scott: Yes, *Carly's Wish*.

TT: And you're about to head off across country on a book tour to promote it…

DS: Yes, starting next week.

TT: Now this comes as we approach something of a grim milestone in Carly's case. In a little over a week, it'll be ten years since she disappeared, at just six years old, from the Fort George State Park.

DS: That's right. On the 15th.

TT: And, if you don't mind me asking, what will you be doing on the 15th? It's a dark day, do you have any plans to mark that day?

DS: I'm doing a reading and a signing in Vegas that night. I'll be doing what I've been doing every day since Carly was taken, talking about the case and my search for her.

TT: I can't imagine, as a parent, how I would feel in your shoes. I feel like I might crawl into a hole, just shut down, disappear from everything, but… somehow you've, for want of a better word, you've, er, thrived, been driven by this. I mean, this is your second book, the first was a best seller, adapted for a movie starring Tom Selleck, the case was featured on *Unsolved Mysteries*. I've heard that HBO is planning a series adaptation later this year. What does *Carly's Wish*, the follow-up to *Carly's Dream*, bring to all this?

DS: Well, I guess people will have to read my book to find out.

TT: Er, I suppose that's true.

Bob Erskine: So, David, we've talked before. This isn't the first time you've been on our show, and we've discussed most of the theories of the case. The main three, I'd say. Does the new book detail any new theories? I'm sure our listeners would love to hear if any new information has come to light.

DS: *Carly's Wish* documents the past five years, my search for Carly in the time since *Carly's Dream* was published and the case first got any real media attention. I mean outside of here in Maine, that is. I suppose before *Carly's Dream*, I was screaming into a void. Now people listen to what I have to say.

TT: Okay, we're going to go to the phones now, but before we do, can I ask what *Carly's Wish*, your new novel's title, refers to?

DS: To Carly wanting to come home. That's her wish, obviously, to come home.

TT: Well, the switchboard is buzzing, let's go to our first caller…

Texts sent from David Scott's phone.

SUNDAY, 8th MAY. 11:08 PM.

DAVID SCOTT:

> Usual waste of time. True Crime kooks and rubberneckers mainly, a few kind old dears, and some fuckwit reading tea leaves. Fucking tea leaves.

GIL CRAWFORD (DAVID'S AGENT):

> What? Who even makes tea with leaves nowadays?

DAVID SCOTT:

> Kooks. Did you hear from Kaplan?

GIL CRAWFORD:

> They'll cover your stay in Vegas, if you set aside the afternoon of the 14th to talk to the documentary crew.

DAVID SCOTT:

> Good. Speak in the morning.

Walt squinted at the number on the cell. He held it closer to the pickup's cabin light and checked it against the email printout. He didn't want to admit it, but he was getting to the age where he needed a phone with an old-man-sized screen, as his daughter liked to tease him.

"Fifty-two is not old," he told her, but right now his eyes begged to differ. He dialed the number. As he waited for it to be answered, he watched a moth bounce along the windshield, trying to get to the light inside.

"Hello?" The voice answering was rough, woken by the call.

"Hello? Is this Mr. Scott? David Scott?"

"What? Yes. Who is this? Do you know what time it is?"

"I am so sorry. I'm travelling interstate" Walt lied. "Isn't it eight a.m. where you are?"

"Uh, no, it's just after four in the morning. Who is this?"

"I heard you on the Crime Time podcast." Walt watched the moth beat against the windshield, fall away, and fly into it again. It wasn't taking *no* for an answer.

At the other end of the line, David sighed. "Okay, look, I don't know how you got my number…"

"Your agent gave it to me. Mr. Crawford."

"Alright, listen, if you've got a tip, call the police, please. If you read some coffee grounds or something like that, call a priest."

"Ten years ago, I watched a man drag a six-year-old girl out of the woods at the Fort George State Park and into his car. I thought she was likely his daughter, but it was odd enough that I followed them."

Walt didn't wait for David to reply. He ended the call. He wound down his window and took a deep drag of the cold morning air. *You don't get fresher than Maine air,* he thought. Not that he'd ever really left the state in his fifty-two years. He threw the phone out onto the verge. It landed face up, the screen blinking on when David called back. Walt flicked off the cabin light and started the pickup. As he drove away, he wondered if the moth would be drawn to the glow from David's call.

Don Gilbert took the cell phone out of the display cabinet behind the counter. He locked it again but didn't bother to take the key from the lock. Small-town security. He placed the box down on the countertop and then turned it over again to find the barcode.

"You starting some kind of criminal enterprise?" he asked Walt. "This is the second one of these cell phones you've bought from me in the past two weeks."

"Don, if I'd taken to a life of crime, don't you think I'd drive a better pickup?"

"Well, you got me there. I was watching a documentary on the, you know, er, *Discovery Crime*, or something. This hitman, when they catch him, he's got four, or was it five, different cell phones. Never made more than one or two calls on 'em before he threw them out. No one could trace him."

"'Cept the police who caught him, I guess."

"Haha, yep, that's true."

"I took the last one fishing with me. Next time you're out on Jackson Lake, if you're lucky you might just reel it in. Fell out of my pocket, over the side the boat, and that was that. And my Kelly wants me to get one of those expensive contract phones, you know, with the big screen. What am I going to do with one of those? Buy some of those Kryptonite Coin things?"

"I hear ya. You say hello to Kelly and to Meg for me, will ya?"

"Will do, Don."

MONDAY, 9th MAY. 11:12 AM.

GIL CRAWFORD:

> Not since that private detective. And I wouldn't again. Not without talking to you first. Why?

DAVID SCOTT:

> Got an odd call at 4am this morning. They said you gave them my number.

GIL CRAWFORD:

Not me. 4am? What did they want?

Tea leaves?

Lol.

?

DAVID SCOTT:

It was just weird. I'll call you when I get to the signing.

David slipped his cell into his jacket pocket and disappeared back inside his house.

Walt had parked his pickup across the street from David's gated house. He'd watched him ferrying luggage from the house into the trunk of his

silver Lexus. From the open trunk lid, he knew he'd
be returning with more packing soon. Walt
wondered how much David's place was worth. A
million dollars? More? How much did a bestseller
and a TV movie go for these days?

David appeared again, weighted down with a
large overnight bag, trying to keep hold of a box
filled to the brim with books. Walt hit the green call
button on the disposable cell and waited.

David half dropped, half spilled the box
of *Carly's Wish* hardbacks into the Lexus's trunk. The
overnight bag followed them in. Walt watched David
fumble the phone from his jacket, and then he hung
up.

Walt waited another ten minutes, until the
driveway gate opened and David was driving down
towards the street, before he called again. The Lexus
stopped where Walt could see David clearly.

"Do you want to know what I saw that day?"
Walt asked.

"Of course I do."

"It'll cost you $5,000. Bring it to Fort George
State Park tomorrow."

Walt could hear the disgust in David's voice.

"You think you're the first person to ask for
money to tell me what happened to my daughter?
How many times in the past ten years do you think
I've heard the same *clues* recycled from true crime
forums? The dreams of amateur psychics? My own

fucking book read back to me? How many times do you think someone's put a price tag on the truth about my daughter—"

"I don't know what happened to your daughter."

"What?"

"I just know where she went. Where she was taken. You want to know, you'll bring the money and be waiting for me at five a.m."

"I could just call the police right now…"

"And tell them what? That you don't care what happened to your daughter? After ten fucking years, I'd be begging to know. Five a.m. tomorrow. $5,000." Walt hung up.

He left David sitting in his driveway. If he was being honest, he had a hard time looking at David. He had a lot more to say, but that would have to wait until they were face to face. On the way home, Walt stopped at Jackson Lake. He walked to the end of one of the jetties and threw the cell into the water. He imagined Don Gilbert hooking it next time he was fishing out there, pulling it, bewildered, into his boat. On a normal day, that might have made him smile, but right now he felt that there was very little to smile about.

Meeting at five a.m. meant by the time they got moving the sun would be rising, and David would see everything Walt wanted to show him. It meant they'd almost certainly be the only ones in the parking lot. It also meant that David would be unlikely to see Walt watching him from the tree line when he drove into the lot. If, of course, he came.

David pulled in at 4:56.

Walt kept him waiting until ten after five before stepping from the trees and onto the gravel parking lot. Ten years is a long time to keep a secret. Another quarter of an hour wasn't going to change the truth.

Walt knocked on the Lexus' rear windshield as he approached. The sound of knuckles on glass set David spinning around. For a moment, Walt thought he was going to bolt. Instead, he watched Walt's wiry figure shuffle along the side of his car and come to a stop by his door.

After a time, David wound down his window. Walt guessed he'd been taking that time to rehearse what he was going to say.

"Well, I'm here." David gestured to an envelope on the passenger seat next to him. "That's your money. You want it, you tell me what you saw that day."

"No."

"What?"

"I'm going to show you. Hand over your phone."

"Why?"

"Because I'm pretty sure you're recording this, and I don't want to star in your next book. Hand it over."

"I'm not going anywhere with you."

"Okay." Walt turned and began to walk away.

"No, wait…I—"

Walt stopped, "Look, mister, you can sit there and hem and haw about this, but I start work in just over an hour and a half, and so if we don't get going soon, we really ain't going anywhere."

"A…Alright, okay." David reached into his jacket pocket and took out his iPhone. He handed it to Walt. Sure enough, a sound graph scrolling across the screen, with a timer running above it, indicated that David's phone was recording.

"I, er…" David fumbled to explain himself.

"I don't care. Of course you were going to record me. But you'll just have to remember what I said for your next book, okay? Now"—Walt handed the phone back—"turn off the recorder."

"What?"

"I don't know how your damn phone works. Just turn it off. And delete the recording."

David took the phone back. He hesitated, wondering if he switched out of the app it'd keep running in the background.

It was too risky. He decided to do as he'd been told. He stopped the recording, deleted what he'd captured, and closed the app.

"Alright. Leave your phone in your car."

Walt waited. He'd expected David to argue, but instead he sat looking up at him. Maybe he was weighing his options. After a time, David opened his glovebox and slipped his iPhone inside.

"Follow me." Walt could sense David's reluctance as he climbed out of his car. *Good*, he thought. "And bring the envelope."

The sky above them had begun to lighten. As they crossed the parking lot, a whip-poor-will lamented the arrival of dawn, calling close by in the woods.

"You ever seen one?" Walt asked.

"What?"

"A whip-poor-will. Often heard, but seldom seen, isn't that what they say? If you hear one, then something bad is gonna happen to you. Of course that's bullshit, otherwise bad things would have happened to most everyone I know."

"I don't believe in that sort of superstitious rubbish."

"Yeah you do. Remember, in your first book, *Carly's Dream*. You said that a day or so before she disappeared, she told you she had a dream she was in a dark place and couldn't get out. It was maybe a cellar or a trunk, you wrote. Not sure why you called that a dream. Sounds like a nightmare to me."

"Like the entire past ten years then, huh?" David lit a smoke, drew deeply on it. Walt had left the parking lot and wandered onto a track heading into the woods.

"That scene in the movie, when that girl actress was trapped in the trunk and she could hear the guy approaching. Holy cow, I barely slept for a week after that. It didn't happen though, did it?"

"It was a movie, they take liberties with the truth."

"Not the *movie*. The dream in your book. You made that up, didn't you?"

David took another deep drag. He looked off into the woods. "Where are we going?"

"Did you even write that book yourself? I heard when you get a deal with a big New York publisher, they set you up with one of those ghostwriters who does the work for you, you just put your name on it."

"Are we going somewhere or just talking?"

"Haha! I knew it! I wish someone would go to work for me." Walt left the track and began to trudge through the brush. "Careful here, it's treacherous," he called back to David.

On the track, the first grey light of the morning had begun to bleed through the canopy above. As they left the dirt path and headed into the woods, thick branches twined above, holding in the night for a while longer yet.

"Where are we going?" David asked again.

"We're taking a shortcut."

"It doesn't feel like it." David ducked under a low branch. His ankle rolled as he put his foot down on the uneven ground and he almost lost his balance. "Shit!"

Walt called from ahead, "Here we are."

They'd arrived at a smaller parking lot. A wooden post-and-rail fence bordered three sides, a dirt track led away on the fourth. Walt clambered over the fence and crossed the lot to his pickup.

"Ten years ago, I was parked up here, along with a couple of other cars. I saw a man drag a young girl out of the woods" —he pointed— "coming from that direction. There wasn't a fence there then."

"I didn't even know this lot was here."

"It's not for the public. It's meant for the rangers. This used to be where people came if, you know, they didn't want to be disturbed."

"What were you doing here then?"

"Get in the pickup."

David joined Walt in the truck.

"Back then, I was a recovering alcoholic. By recovering, I mean I was out here drinking. Guy strides right past the front of my truck. Maybe he hadn't noticed I was sat here, maybe he didn't care. He pretty much throws the girl into his car." He pointed again. "It was parked there. He guns his engine and gets the hell out of here."

David took out another smoke.

"Don't light that in here."

Sheepishly, David put the cigarette away. "What happened next?"

"Well, I was pretty out of it, wasn't entirely sure what I'd seen, thought maybe it was a father and his little girl, you know how kids throw tantrums. They can scream blue murder. But, no, something felt off. So, I followed them."

Walt started up the pickup and pulled out of the lot.

They drove the dirt track in silence, the pickup rocking and jolting over the uneven road. Walt drove the track like he knew it, too fast for David, who clung on to the grab handle above him. Eventually they arrived at a wooden gate, propped open, and beyond that, to David's relief, the rough road turned to asphalt, and they left the woods behind.

"I heard you on that Crime Time podcast—"

"You told me that. Where are you taking me?" They'd left the track, but David still held on to the handle.

"You've done a lot of talking over the past ten years. A whole lot of talking."

"What's your point?"

"How much *looking* have you actually done yourself?"

"It's not that simple."

"Like that day in the park. What were you looking for then?"

"What?"

"I heard it was tail. That you'd arranged to meet up with a woman there."

"They printed that in the *Herald* just after my first book came out. That's not new information."

"Still, you took your six-year-old to a park so you could hook up with some pussy."

"That's not how it was. I don't have to explain myself to you."

"You do if you want me to tell you what I know." Walt slowed the pickup. He peered out of his driver's side window into the tree line. A break in the trees revealed an overgrown track.

"Nah, I don't think that's it."

Walt continued on.

"Do you actually know where we're going?"

"It's been ten years, okay? Things have changed. So, what were you doing in the woods that day? *Hiking?* That's what you told the police at first, isn't it?"

"Look, it wasn't just some random hookup, okay? We'd been talking online for months."

"Well, that makes all the difference."

"Okay, look, my marriage was failing. My wife, she drank. She drank a lot. She was an alcoholic. It was…"

"Wait…" Walt looked off to the right. "This looks promising." He swung the pickup off the highway in a way that made David glad he was still holding the grab handle.

They'd turned onto a partially graveled road. "Yeah, this is it. I followed the car along here. Your wife's dead now, though, right? Drank herself into the ground, huh?"

"Why are you showing me this now?" David scanned their surroundings, "Why didn't you come forward when Carly first disappeared?"

"I didn't need the money then. I need it now."

"That's it?" David spun around. "You knew what happened to my daughter, and you didn't come forward because you couldn't make a buck out of it?" He grabbed at Walt's shirt.

"Look, I already told you, I don't know what happened. I just know where she went. Now, you can either sit back, shut the fuck up, and I'll take you there. Or if you want a fight, I'll kick your ass and leave you by the side of the road. Which is it to be?"

"I...I'm armed, you know." David had already dropped his hand away, though. He leaned back in his seat.

"Why? Are you afraid the truth's gonna hurt you?"

Ahead, the road twisted a sharp left. Walt followed it around, and in the clearing before them was the house.

The old clapboard house had likely been white once. Now its boards were the color of bones, shrunk and split from years of neglect. Mold had spread across them like decay between stained, old teeth.

Walt pulled up and killed the engine. "This is it. This is where I followed them to."

David looked from Walt to the house. The porch had partially collapsed. Its sagging eave reminded David of a drooping eyelid.

"They went inside there." Walt wound down his window. The cool morning air made his skin prickle. "I had other stuff I had to do and so I left."

"You did *what*? Why would you do that? Wasn't it obvious that something was wrong?"

"I told you. I had other things I needed to get done."

"You're lying! You just drove me out here for the money, didn't you? Admit it! You heard me on the podcast and thought you could make a quick buck."

"No. But I don't much care if you believe me or not. That's what happened, and that's your five grand of information. Now pay up and get out. I can't sit here talking to you all day."

"No, you're lying. You have to be! If you'd seen what you said, you'd have reported it, surely. You'd have told someone before now, when there's nothing that can be done." David grabbed at the passenger door handle and threw the door open.

"Look, I told you what I saw. I told you what happened. I might've sat here for another ten, maybe fifteen minutes after they went in. Didn't see anything else, didn't hear anything."

"I have to go inside"

David was already half out the door. Walt sighed. "Yeah, I thought you might say that."

"And I'm taking your money. You want it, you'll come with me."

Walt hung back, watching David stumble through the knee-high grass as he headed for the house. He hadn't lied about what happened ten years before. He *had* sat in his pickup outside this house. He'd even parked pretty much where his truck was now. He sighed, kicked at the dirt caught in the pickup's treads, and then began to trudge through the long grass after David.

The house's windows were shuttered. They'd been closed the last time Walt had been there, too. *See no evil,* he thought.

David leaned close to the flaking slats, trying to look between the boards and see inside. He forced his fingers under one of the shutters and pulled at it. A stream of dark sludge slithered off the sill, drooling over David's hand and down the front of the house. Likely rain, blown in and trapped by the warped shutters; its dark appearance and stench made David think of something putrefying.

"Christ!" he snatched his hand away, wiping it on his pants.

"Maybe we should try the door," suggested Walt.

A tattered fly screen was latched shut over the front door. Its gauze had long since parted company with the frame. It likely hadn't stopped a fly in years. Walt pulled the screen open. David tried the door. It swung back into a hallway the color of nicotine.

A stained towel had been thrown onto the bare boards of the entrance hall. Like the outside of the house, mold had begun to spread over it.

David leaned into the hallway. He stopped, listening, feeling incredibly vulnerable. At any moment, someone could rush at him from one of the doorways off the corridor.

The house remained silent.

David stepped inside. Walt followed.

They moved through the house without speaking. Each room they passed seemed to be more chaotic than the last. In one, possibly a living room, vinyl flooring had been pulled up and rolled back to reveal the filthy boards beneath. Against the wall, newspapers had been stacked from floor to ceiling. A dark bloom of mold spread from the stacked papers across the yellowed tiles above. *Everything is rotten here,* thought David.

Walt stepped around a pile of empty food cans that

had been built into a pyramid in the middle of the hallway.

Where there wasn't detritus, there was dust. The air was thick with it. Walt held his shirt cuff over his mouth and nose. The way David moved in fits and starts, Walt could tell he was close to turning tail and running.

When he'd unlocked the house that morning, before heading to meet David at the park, he'd considered that David might not have the nerve to go inside, that he might take more leading, more motivation than Walt's story provided. If he turned to bolt before they arrived at the locked door ahead, Walt's plan would have to change.

They passed a kitchen, a bedroom where a mattress had been propped up against a single bedframe like a kid's makeshift fort. Underneath, more mold-covered newspaper, and a bowl a dog might've eaten from. A rope had been tied to one of the legs of the bed, its other end lay frayed beneath the fort.

"Dear God…" David choked out the words.

The tub in the bathroom was filled with more half-eaten food cans, jagged metal edges glimmering where they'd been pried open, and their contents spilled and smeared over the plastic.

Ahead, David stopped in his tracks. A door off the corridor had been fitted with a large padlock.

The heads of the screws holding the hasp in place stood out from the metal plate, allowing David to open the door a crack before they stopped his progress. He rattled the door against its lock.

"I think I can open this. Can you give me a hand?" David leaned against the door.

Walt had loosened the screws himself. They were about to find out if he'd loosened them enough.

The two men shoved against the door. The first time, the hasp held. They shoved again, and with the sound of splintering wood, the door was thrown open. It slammed back into the bare brick wall behind it, revealing a set of wooden stairs falling away into the darkness ahead.

David rocked forward on the top step. Walt grabbed the back of his jacket and held him.

"Thanks." David put a hand on the doorframe to steady himself. Walt continued to hold onto his jacket.

"Is it really concern for you daughter that brought you here?" Walt's grip tightened.

"What?"

"I mean, if she's dead, if she died ten years ago, she doesn't give a fuck about your search, does she? She can't."

"What are you saying?"

David tried to shake Walt's hand off his back. Walt held firm.

"Or is it guilt driving you? That you left your daughter with another kid younger than her, with your date's little boy, while you took your friend for a *walk* in the woods."

"Fuck you. You don't know me." David pulled against Walt's grip.

Walt looked past David, down into the darkness ahead of them. They could both smell the metallic stench rising from the cellar.

Walt waited for David to buck against his grip one last time before he let him go. The father tottered on the top step.

"Maybe you're right," Walt continued. "I guess I've only really *heard* about you until now. You want me to leave? I'll take my money and go, if you like."

David didn't answer. He swept a nervous hand over the cold brick wall, feeling for a light switch. He found it and flicked it.

Nothing.

He took a hesitant step forward. Walt followed him down.

With each step, the stench grew stronger. Behind David, Walt retched. They'd soon left behind what little muted light the house offered.

They leaned against the cold cellar wall, fingers slipping over the damp bricks, feet cautiously finding the wooden steps, testing the warped wood before putting their weight down upon them.

David stepped onto the soil floor of the cellar. He felt the earth slip and give under his weight. His shoe sank into the wet ground. Behind him, there was a click as Walt switched on the flashlight he'd been carrying in his shirt pocket.

"Seriously, you had that on you the whole—" David's words died as he saw where Walt's flashlight beam had stopped. "Oh, dear God."

In the corner of the cellar, slumped against the wall, was a corpse.

David raced over to the body, although it was more of a pile of bones wrapped in rags. He skidded, almost falling onto the remains.

Even wasted to nearly nothing, it was clear that the body had once been an adult. The bones were too large to be a child's. David grabbed at the clothes, pulling them away from the wall, scattering the bones across the floor. Maybe he expected to find something beneath the body, maybe it was just panic driving him. He spun away from the wall, frantically searching the cellar floor around him. Walt tried to follow David, light his way with the flashlight. That didn't stop David from tripping over the shattered remains of an ornamental owl statue. He lost his footing and slammed down into the mud.

Walt helped David back to the stairs and sat him down.

"She's not down here. It's just him."

"How? How do you know that?"

"Well, I lied to you."

"What?"

"I lied to you to get you here. And I lied when we were in the truck just now."

"I…I don't understand."

"I did follow him and Carly from the park. I followed them the way we drove, out to this house. I watched them, like I told you, watched him drag her inside. I sat in my truck, smoked a cigarette, and… I almost left. But I didn't. I followed them into this house."

Walt wandered over to the owl statue. He pulled its considerable weight from the mud. One of the owl's wings had been smashed off.

"Coming up the corridor, I could hear them down here. I could hear her fighting him, trying to fight him off. He's making this weird, whining sound, halfway between a child and some kind of an animal. Then there's this thud. Stopped me dead. You know, the kind of sound that just screams something's wrong. After that she wasn't fighting him anymore."

Carrying the statue, Walt crossed back to David.

"Well, I picked up the first thing that came to hand. This fucking owl statue. Weighs a damn ton. I almost dropped it down the stairs. I'm not sure how I did it, but I managed to get pretty close to him before he realized I was there. He's got his pants round his ankles, down on his hands and knees in front of where she's laying. And he's making that noise, only it's getting louder, louder and he's getting ready to… Christ, to do whatever goddam awful thing he was planning to do to her. And, for a moment, I thought *he's an animal*, he's an animal somehow dressed in a man's skin. How could he not have been seen for what he was when he was in that park? How did he manage to walk among the rest of the people there and not be spotted, not be seen for what he really was?"

Walt held the statue with white knuckles. "I took this statue, and I brought it down on his head. I brought it down again and again. He scuttled into that corner, whimpering and holding his hands up, trying to protect himself. Well, that just made me angrier. I hit him so hard that I snapped the damn wing off this thing. I remember hearing the bone in his arm crack, it bent awkwardly, like an arm shouldn't, and just fell useless to his side. I smashed his skull until I was covered in his animal blood. Until he was barely recognizable as either a man or a beast."

David's voice was a hoarse croak. "What? What happened…"

"Carly was on the floor, over there." Walt pointed with the remaining wing of the statue, "He'd cracked her head pretty bad. I scooped her up, carried her out of here, put her in my pickup, and I drove away."

"What?" David tried to stand up, but Walt pushed him back onto the stair. "What happened? Was she dead? What did you do with her? Tell me! You have to tell me!"

"No. No, I don't. While all this was happening, what were you doing? Chasing pussy? I don't think you'd even realized she was gone by the time I was picking her up off of this floor."

"What? Please… What did you do to her? Why didn't you bring her back?"

"Yeah, I thought about it. I watched you giving a press conference that evening. The one at the park, with all the cops gathered around you. Remember? You were talking when you should have been out there looking. Talking, like you've done for the past ten years."

"What did you do to her?"

"She told me about those nights when you left her, left her with a mother who could barely look after herself, let alone a six-year-old. What were you doing those nights?"

"Please. What did you do with her?"

"She said you'd roll in late, if you came home at all, drunk and whispering on your phone, arranging your next date. She used to lay awake listening."

"Are you telling me she's alive? You bastard! What have you done with her?"

"I didn't do anything with her. I let her decide what she wanted to do. That's what I've done for the past ten years. And that's why we're here today."

"What do you mean? You've got to tell me where she is!"

"No. I'm not going to do that. I'm here because she asked me to give you a message."

"What?" David was on his feet now. "What message?"

"You should have been a better father." Walt struck David with the owl statue. The blow knocked David back onto the stairs. He threw up his hands to try and deflect the blows, but they were useless against Walt's strikes. Walt brought the statue down again and again until there was no doubt that David was dead.

Walt had bought several padlocks from Don Gilbert's store over the past few months. He fitted a fresh one to the outside of the cellar door. He fitted another on the front door of the house. He hoped he'd never have to set foot in that foul place again. After that, he drove to a motel, where he rented a room for cash and showered for the best part of an hour.

Kelly was sitting on the porch bench when Walt pulled the pick-up into the driveway of their small house. She'd chosen the name Kelly herself. It was close enough to Carly that she'd thought it'd be easy to get used to.

Walt joined her on the bench. "Here." He passed her the envelope with David's five thousand dollars in it.

"I don't want this."

"I know. But I'm gonna hold on to it for you, case you change your mind."

"It's done then?"

"Yeah."

"Thank you. I couldn't stand to listen to him anymore."

"I know."

"Ten years of whining how he loved me so much. Podcasts, television, that awful movie, like he was the fucking victim in all this. If he'd loved me so much, he wouldn't have lost me in the first place."

"THE GRAVE LISTENERS"

Growing up, my friend, Cole, was completely obsessed with our local cemetery. Well, actually with the idea that someone was gonna get buried alive in our local cemetery. So much so, that whenever anyone was buried there, he'd go out later that day, or in the evening, to listen. He told us how he'd place his head down, ear to the recently turned earth, listening for any sounds.

Yeah, Cole was a bit of an oddball. His mom and dad were doctors, eccentric types, always had the latest copy of the *National Geographic* magazine on their coffee table when I went over to his house. It was in one of those magazines that he'd read about a spate of premature burials in Johannesburg. People heard knocking, screaming from their freshly dug graves.

This is back before the internet and mobile phones. The world seemed like a much larger place back then. Especially to a group of naïve ten-year-old boys. If people were getting buried alive in

Johannesburg (none of us were exactly sure where that was), surely they could be getting buried alive in a small Texas town in the '80s.

Cole was an oddball, sure, but he was persuasive too. And it wasn't long before we were going on his vigils as a group. We called our team "The Grave Listeners," which was meant to make us sound cool like the Ghostbusters, but just made us sound like we took everything way too seriously.

We spent hours with our heads down, ears literally to the ground, listening for any sound that might come from the recently buried beneath us. Every now and then one of the team would raise a hand to shush the rest of the us. We'd all listen extra intently for the seconds that followed...

But then that hand would waver and drop as it became clear it was a mistake. One time, Sam's hand shot up into the air. We all listened, hushed and breath held. Then he let rip a huge fart and we all fell about. We were still laughing as we packed up that night.

It didn't take long for us to realize that listening with our heads pressed to the ground might not be the best way to hear if anything was happening beneath us. Six feet is a lot of earth for sound to travel through. So Cole came up with a plan.

He *borrowed* one of his dad's old stethoscopes, took it apart, and jury-rigged a longer piece of tubing between the earpiece and the 'bit that's always freezing when they put it on your chest at the doctor's."

Plan was, that we'd dig a hole in the soil, drop in the listening end, and not only would we be able to hear more clearly, but we'd be closer to the coffin, too. I had to admit, it was a pretty clever idea. We waited for the next burial to take place so we could try it out.

If we'd known who the next person in our town to be buried would be, none of us would have been wishing the time away.

About a week later, Sam, Doug and I were called into the Principal's office. Cole hadn't turned in that morning. Principal Mosley sat us down and we found out why. The evening before, Cole's mom had been cooking dinner when she'd screamed, clamped her hands to her chest, and dropped down dead. I remember we sat in horrified silence, then Doug started to cry. We'd known Mrs. B. our whole lives. It was just awful.

The funeral was later that week, and I think that most of the town must have turned out for it. I barely got to see Cole for all the well-wishers who swarmed around his dad and him. I just remember his red eyes and how he looked so lost and confused.

I stood next to Doug, and Sam was on the opposite side of the grave at the committal. As we watched the coffin being lowered into the ground, our eyes met. I knew right away what they were thinking.

We didn't tell Cole what we had planned. We were going to do this for him, so he didn't have to. At the wake, Doug kept watch while I snuck up to Cole's room to grab the stethoscope. It was on his desk. As I turned around, I saw that he had a photograph of his mom and him, lying next to his pillow on his bed. I started crying so hard I had to hide in the bathroom until I'd pulled myself together.

That evening, we met up at Mrs. B.'s grave. Doug said a prayer, out of respect, then Sam used a stick to bore a hole into the earth so we could drop the listening end of the stethoscope in. We took turns to wear the headphones.

It all kicked off around 7.30pm. Doug was crouching by the grave, listening and reading a Spiderman comic with a torch, when suddenly he shoots up a hand to shush us. A split second later, he pulls the headphones out of his ears, tries to stand up but falls back on his ass. All the time he's shaking his head. "No, no, no way."

Sam and I tried to get out of him what he'd heard, but by then he'd found his feet and he ran.

It took a good couple of minutes for me to get up the nerve to put the headphones on after that. All the time, the shadows in the cemetery grew longer around us.

Scratching. What Doug had heard was scratching. Slow, determined scratching, coming from the earth beneath us. I heard it too. And just like Doug, I hauled myself to my feet and I ran. Pulled the stethoscope clean out of the ground and ran with it still hanging from my ears. Didn't stop running until we made it to Sam's house.

The next day, the police were called to Mrs. B.'s grave. The story made the local paper. Something, maybe an animal, vandals most likely, had been digging around in the freshly lain earth. It was a heck of a mess. We hadn't left it that way.

That afternoon, I rode up to Cable Point with the stethoscope and threw it off. I didn't ever want to listen to another grave after that night.

A few weeks passed, and Cole didn't seem to be coping at all with his mom's death. I arranged for us all to meet up at Sam's and play *Elite* on his dad's computer. Cole loved *Elite*. But even that didn't seem to raise his spirits. He just looked so exhausted.

Later, while we were waiting for our dads to pick us up, I asked him if there was anything I could do. He thanked me but told me it wasn't just his mom's passing that was keeping him up at night, it was the scratching. Said he heard it every night, sometimes at the doors, sometimes against the glass of his bedroom window. As if something outside were trying to claw its way in.

"THE BONE MAN OF
SANATORIUM LAKE."
(Macedon Ranges, Melbourne, Australia.)

I've got a friend who used to work for Parks Victoria. I say *used to*, as he's retired now. That was one of the conditions of me telling you about his experiences around Sanatorium Lake. I had to wait until he'd clocked off for the last time before writing about it. I'll tell you why soon enough.

For the purpose of this account, I'm going to refer to my friend as Phil. That's not his real name. That was another condition of his letting me tell you about what happened to him.

I met Phil not long after I moved from the UK to Melbourne in 2014. I got a job working in a local pub, and Phil and his wife were some of our Saturday night regulars. They'd eat dinner, then have a few drinks and play the pokies for a couple of hours afterwards. It was a small pub in a small town, so, unless there was an event on, most of our Saturday night trade was over by about 8.30 in the evening. That left plenty of time for talking to the few regulars who hung back. That's how I got to know Phil.

There's kind of an unwritten rule in Australia that the more someone takes the piss out of you, the more they actually like you. Phil and his wife used to give me hell. We had a lot of laughs on those Saturday nights. So, when he first mentioned Sanatorium Lake, I thought he was just joking. He knew I liked horror, and so I thought the whole thing was going to lead up to a punchline. But it didn't.

He changed the subject pretty quickly after first bringing it up. It was his birthday and he'd had skinful, so I didn't really think much of it. I thought he was just trying to come up with a better joke.

About six months later, I'm over at Phil's house, and in the den he's got a map of the Macedon Regional Park. That's his park, his patrol area. He said he gets moved around a bit, particularly if there's a concert on at Hanging Rock, but he's mainly based at the park. He loves it, says it's the best office you could hope to have.

I'm looking over the map, and I'm picking out spots I know—Hanging Rock, Mount Macedon— and on the right hand side, I spot a small patch of blue: Sanatorium Lake. So I make a joke, I say "What about the horror that lurks in Sanatorium Lake?" I'm thinking he might finally tell me the rest of that joke he started back in the pub on his birthday. Only he doesn't. In fact, he kind of clams up. He heads out of the den, comes back a minute later with two fresh beers (neither of us had finished the last one), hands one to me, and then sits down and starts to tell the story I'm about to recount.

Now, Phil's a big guy, rugby player when he was younger, bit of a gym junkie in later life, he looks how I imagine an outdoorsman should. Even in his mid-fifties, he looked like he could handle most things the outdoors might throw at him. But that night, sitting in his den, drinking a beer too fast, he just looked haunted.

1. The Hiker.

Phil joined Parks Victoria back in early 2008. He'd worked as a ranger in NSW, but when his wife was offered a much better-paying job in Melbourne, they upped sticks and moved.

On starting at the park, Phil was assigned a mentor ranger (Ray), to show him around. Ray was six months off from his retirement. The plan was, that they'd work together for those last six months and then Phil would take over Ray's responsibilities full time.

It didn't take Phil long to work out that there were areas of the park that Ray didn't like going to after dark. He told me how, when they were on a night shift together, Ray would make sure they started out at Sanatorium Lake, when it was still dusk, and then not go back that way again until the end of their shift. This was even though it was on a route they were meant to patrol several times over the course of the night.

So, Phil decides he's going to ask some of the other rangers about this.

"It's because of the hiker," they tell him. *Really,* thinks Phil. He's worked as a ranger for most of his adult life, and he knows that all parks have their legends; and almost all of those legends are bullshit. Also, Phil's the new guy. So, he wonders if all this is leading to some kind of initiation practical joke.

They tell him that a body was found in the undergrowth, off the track to Sanatorium Lake.

To get to the lake, you have to park at a parking lot and walk. There's not a road up to the water. It's a track through the forest, lots of Eucalyptus trees and large ground cover ferns. That's probably why the body wasn't found right away.

It'd been out there for over a week. It was late summer, and animals had gotten to it before a bushwalker found the remains when they wandered off the track to take a piss. Ray was on duty that evening, got a hysterical call from the guy. He found him almost passed out, collapsed on the edge of the track. Ray said the poor guy had thrown up all over himself, was shaking so bad he could barely speak. When Ray got to the body, he could see why.

It's not the sort of thing that you ever forget.

The police said that the remains belonged to a hiker who'd, most likely, gotten hit by a car out on the main road. It's a winding, thin road up towards the parking lot, easy to be surprised as you turn a bend, especially if you're going too fast. Horribly, it seemed like someone had hit the hiker and driven off. At least, that was what the police concluded. You see, the bottom half of the body was a mess. One leg was completely missing, the other mangled until it was near unrecognizable. The pelvis had been smashed to a pulp.

They surmised that the hiker had been run over, and dragged themselves off the road and into the brush where they'd died. The thing is, it's not just a few feet from the road to Sanatorium Lake. It's a good 200-plus meters. That's over 600 feet. How someone that badly injured could drag themselves all that way, well, it seemed extremely unlikely. Then there was the shoe.

The left leg of the hiker was completely gone, torn out of the socket at the pelvis. The right leg was a shattered, twisted mess, but on the barely attached right foot was an Adidas hiking shoe. Two weeks after the body was found, the left shoe was found floating in Sanatorium Lake.

Well, Phil still suspected that he was being pranked, so he went home and did a bit of googling. Sure enough (it's pretty easy to find in a Google search), a body had been found in the brush not far from Sanatorium Lake. There wasn't any mention of the shoe in the articles he read. He thought that might have been added by the other rangers for effect. What he did find, though, was a bunch of ghost-hunting sites with articles on the lake. Reports from night vigils, with photographs of the trees lit up by a camera flash, orbs caught in the shots… *Probably mozzies*, he thought. There was even some low quality night vision video of a bunch of kids freaking out at the sound of wood cracking close by them.

On another site, he found an article on the history of the lake.

"Sanatorium Lake is a man-made lake. It was constructed in 1899 to supply water to a tuberculosis sanatorium that was planned to be built nearby. Only the plans for the hospital were abandoned, and that's where the legend of the lake begins. One account has it that Aboriginal workers hired to work on the site refused to even go near it, due to "the amount of spirits" they sensed around the lake. Another has it that, when they were digging the lake, they found something buried in the dirt beneath it: "Remains. Lots of remains."

For the purpose of this piece, I pulled that quote from the website *Paranormal Victoria*. We couldn't find the site that Phil found in 2008, but the story is the same. Aside from this quote, I wasn't able to find anything to suggest either of the referenced accounts are true. Work *was* abandoned on the hospital after the lake was finished. I couldn't find anything to explain why that happened.

Phil told me that he never asked Ray about the evening the hiker was found. He respected Ray's privacy, and did the patrols of Sanatorium Lake on his own. He didn't notice anything odd about the lake or the area surrounding it.

A week before Ray was due to retire, he collapsed while he was cleaning the pool in his back yard. It was a heart attack. His wife found him. She called 000, and did her best to do CPR while she waited for the paramedics to arrive, but by the time they got there, he was already gone.

At the wake, Ray's wife told Phil that she'd spotted him out their bedroom window, sweeping back and forth across the water with the pool skimmer, like he was trying to haul something out. She was on her way to ask him what the hell he was doing when she found him lying collapsed at the poolside. It was the middle of winter. There wasn't anything in the pool.

2. The Boy.

A week after Ray had passed away, the kid went missing.

A couple, with their seven year old son, had been hiking in the woods that border Lions Head Road. They'd wandered off the track, gotten lost, and in an attempt to find their way back to the parking lot, had tried to cross a dried-up creek bed. Only, the husband had slipped and fallen, badly twisting his ankle.

His wife had rushed to help him. After she'd checked her husband was okay, she'd turned back to her son, only to find him gone.

Now, people get lost in the woods all the time. It's a repetitive terrain that's easy to get turned around in. In fact, Phil told me it's probably the most common call for help they get, someone missing from a group. He also said that almost every single time, he'd ask, "Were you on the designated tracks?" and the answer would come back sheepishly, "No."

Most commonly, it's older people who've wandered away from their family and gotten themselves lost. Scariest though, by far, is when kids go missing. It's worse still if that happens later in the day. This call came in around 3pm. Lions Head Road shares its parking lot with Sanatorium Lake.

Phil and the other rangers were doing a sweep of the surrounding area when the CFA[2] arrived to help with the search. The police joined at about the same time. Winters in Victoria are mild compared to what I'm used to in the UK, but it can still get down close to freezing at night, and everyone

---

[2] The Country Fire Authority (CFA) are the Australian (in the state of Victoria) equivalent of the Fire Department. They also help with search and rescue in the way that the National Park Service does.

wanted to find that little boy before the sun went down.

They searched for four hours straight without any luck. It gets dark quickly in the winter, quicker still under the tree canopy. It was a cloudy night, so they didn't even have moonlight to help them. Phil said that with every minute that passed he felt more and more sick to his stomach. He'd taken to walking the shore of Sanatorium Lake, doing laps with the beam of his torch sweeping back and forth over the water. He thought of Ray more than once that night.

It was almost 8pm when the call went up. Someone was shouting from the woods that border the lake. Phil raced into the brush. He found a lone CFA officer standing under a tall Eucalyptus tree with his torch aimed up into branches above. Phil said he swung his torch up and it was like when you see a deer caught in headlights. Two glowing orbs picked out by the beam of light, two wide eyes in a face so white and terrified that Phil almost screamed when he saw it.

The kid had somehow scrabbled up the tree and was clinging on above them. Phil and the CFA officer, Josh, tried to coax him down but he refused to even consider it. He kept asking, "Has he gone yet? Has he gone yet?"

Eventually more CFA officers arrived with a ladder to help bring the boy down. There was no way Phil or Josh could have gotten up to the kid without it. How he'd managed to climb the near bare trunk was beyond the them. Phil told me, "I guess if you're scared enough, you can do some pretty crazy shit."

The kid was reunited with his family and then taken to be interviewed by the police about what had happened. All the time, he was still searching around with those wide, scared eyes. Phil said he was relieved they'd found the boy, but he couldn't help but keep following the kid's gaze, off into the darkness between the trees. Said he couldn't relax until the police had loaded the kid into a car and driven him away from that place. Said that was the night he first began to understand how Ray had felt about the lake.

A few more months go by, and when the weather gets warmer, there's a CFA family day held at the park. They do this a couple of times a year. They have a big barbeque, music, raffles, lots of the CFA families turn up. They're pretty tame events, but the rangers keep an eye to make sure no one gets too merry and decides to go for a drunken hike, or worse, a swim when they'd had a skinful. Anyway, Phil's checking in (grabbing himself a burger, really) when he spots Josh, the CFA officer who found the boy up the tree.

Well, they catch up and Phil asks Josh about that night. Did he get asked to give a statement?

Because the police didn't get in touch with Phil again after they left with the boy. Josh tells him that, yeah, they were going to take his statement, but then the whole thing got dropped.

Apparently, when the kid was being interviewed, he couldn't give a coherent description of the man who'd tried to snatch him, so one of the police officers had the idea to get him to draw what he remembered. They gave him some paper and left him alone with his Dad while he worked on his sketch.

Well, about an hour later, the Dad calls for the officer to come back in. Tells them that the boy was mistaken, there wasn't any man, showed the officer the drawings that the kid had done. In these drawings there's a figure. It's kind of hunched over, like it's an old man. It's got all these arms, maybe three sets of them, and more hanging round its waist. He's drawn the upper body like a skeleton, all exposed bones. Only all these bones are drawn in red.

Basically, he's just drawn some kid's idea of the bogeyman. The officer asks the boy about the drawings. Asks why the man has too many arms. The kid tells him that he takes them. He's got legs, too, he says. Calls him "the bone man." Says he lives in the lake.

It turns out that Mum and Dad's relationship had been in a bad place for a while. There was likely a divorce on the horizon. That, on that afternoon, they were arguing when the husband fell down the ditch. The police concluded that the boy just ran off because he was upset. Then when he saw how much worry he'd caused, he made up a story so he wouldn't get into trouble.

I've spoken to Josh about the night the boy went missing. Him and Phil kept in touch after that barbeque. They both agree that, while the kid might have made the story up, there's no denying that when they found him, he was scared to the point that he'd somehow climbed a tree that neither of the two men (one in his forties, and the other mid-twenties) could get close to scaling.

3. It's Not The Sort Of Thing That You Ever Forget.

Last summer I drove up to Sanatorium Lake. I parked in the Lions Head parking lot, and walked the track through the woods to get to the lake. It's a beautiful place. Still water circled by tall, bare eucalyptus trees. White trunks reflected in the mirror of the lake's surface. And quiet, so quiet. It's easy to understand why people like to hike the track round the lake. I took some photos, tried to find the tree that the boy climbed on that night back in 2008. It's always cooler under the tree canopy, but out by the water it felt unnaturally cold. It was a 30-degree day, and my arms were covered with goosebumps. For the hell of it, I took some shots of the water's surface, pointing my camera out into the middle of the lake. I also shot up into the tree canopy, like the photos I'd seen online when I'd read about paranormal activity at the lake.

I was the only person parked up at the Lions Head parking lot that afternoon. I thought of the hiker, found dead only a few feet from the track I'd just walked. I thought about the kid, about what had really happened to him that night. But more than that, as I flicked though the shots on my camera, I thought of Phil, and the night in 2012 that had been the last time he'd been out to the lake.

If you're a fan of cold cases and unsolved mysteries, then you might already know what I'm talking about here. The summer of 2012 is when Kelly Baxter disappeared from a camping trip in the woods around Sanatorium Lake.

On the night of Jan 15th 2012, just after 5pm, Kelly and a group of her friends (four boys and two other girls) got dropped off on Lions Head Road. You're not supposed to stay at the park at night, so they got a maxi-taxi to drop them before sundown and trekked into the woods, before any of the rangers could spot them. They had camping equipment, food and booze. Almost everything they needed for a night of partying. They'd arranged to meet a dealer later that evening, at a clearing near their camp, to score some weed and ecstasy. The dealer is often cited as one of the prime suspects in Kelly's disappearance.

Kelly disappeared sometime between 1am and 3am on 16th Jan. The police were never able to ascertain an exact time, as the friends panicked when they found Kelly gone, and waited until they'd disposed of the drugs they'd purchased before alerting the rangers that Kelly had disappeared.

By 2012, Phil was working in another part of the park. It's a big area and, every few years, rangers are rotated around to new stations. He joined the search for Kelly a little after 4am. He told me that all that fear he felt in 2008 was back straight away, like it'd been waiting somewhere in the woods for him to return.

The police brought in dogs and specialist trackers, but no sign of Kelly turned up. For three more days, police, rangers and volunteers swept the area around Lions Head Road and Sanatorium Lake. Phil described it as, "Forty, maybe fifty people all holding their breath. No one talking, everyone listening for the smallest sound, hoping a whistle would go off, that someone would shout so we knew they'd found something. But it never happened. Now imagine being her parents. They'll be holding their breath for the rest of their lives."

Even after the search had been called off, rangers would still head out into the wood along Lions Head Road in the hope that they'd stumble across a clue that might help find Kelly. They'd go out there after their shifts, on their days off. Even months afterwards Phil would often find other rangers sweeping through the brush when he went out to search. It became something they did out of respect for the family.

For Phil, his search ended on June 10th that year.

The disappearance had really taken a toll on him. He has daughters himself, and couldn't help but see himself in the broken shells of Kelly's mother and father. He'd see their haunted faces on the Channel 7 news, pleading for answers, and when the article cut to photos of Kelly, he'd see his daughters Chloe and Rachel. That drove him to keep going back to the lake, night after night.

He started drinking more, too. He'd take a six-pack with him, and some nights he'd just sit in the car with his window down, drinking and smoking, listening to the sounds of the park at night. June 10th was a cloudy night, no moon to light up the Lions Head Road parking lot. Phil didn't mind. The darker the night, the more keenly he could hear.

In the end, though, it wasn't a sound that caused him to flee that night.

A little after 11pm, Phil felt a wave of anxiety flood over him. One minute he'd been drinking and calmly listening to the night, the next he was so scared he found himself fumbling for the window control and locking all the doors against the darkness. His heart was slamming, out of control, his chest was suddenly so tight he thought he might be having a heart attack. Then he heard the movement.

Phil sank down in his seat. In the pitch dark, something approached the car.

Shuffling. He could hear the movement drawing nearer. The closer it got, the more Phil's anxiety grew. It drew right up to the passenger door behind him.

Suddenly, it was hammering against the passenger window. A wet thud, thud, thud, that caused Phil to cower in his seat, trying to make himself as small as possible so he wouldn't be seen.

The beating moved around to the back of the car. He could feel it echoing through the trunk. The longer it went on, the more he became sure that it was looking for a way to get in, to get at him.

He somehow found the nerve to grab at the key in the ignition and turn it.

His headlights exploded on. What Phil saw in front of his car made him scream out in horror.

About six feet ahead, caught in the stark light of his headlamps, a figure lurched left and right, stumbling across the parking lot. It wore the same white t-shirt and pants that Phil had seen in the photos of Kelly Baxter, only now great patches of red had spread across the material. Blood from her wounds, he guessed. There was so much blood.

The figure tottered on bare feet. It was standing, barely, even though Phil was certain that what he was seeing was impossible. There was no way it could be alive, not with the wounds it had suffered.

Where the sleeves of Kelly's shirt ended, where her arms should have been, were two raw stumps. On one side, what he at first mistook for the white material of her shirt, he realized was the bone of her upper arm protruding from the flesh.

All the time, wet hands hammered on the back windscreen of Phil's car.

Kelly swayed, and as if she'd become aware that he was watching her, she turned towards Phil. Up to that point, her hair had hidden the worst of the damage to her head.

Phil couldn't take any more, he panicked and slammed his foot down on the accelerator. The car jolted forward. In that same instant, Kelly let out a terrible, mournful wail and disappeared. Phil tore out of the parking lot. He hasn't returned to the Lions Head car park since.

For a long time after that night, Phil tried to convince himself that he'd just fallen asleep in his car. That he'd gotten drunk and dreamed the whole thing. That the smeared handprints on the back passenger window of his car had been there before he'd parked up that evening.

Phil retired from Parks Victoria in 2018. We'd talked about my writing an account of his experiences back in 2015, but initially he point-blank refused. I broached the subject a few more times in the following years, and he eventually agreed with the condition that I wait until he'd retired. He told me that it was one thing to talk about it, share it with me, but putting it down on paper… That somehow made it real. And, if it were real, there would be no way he could go back to the park again.

To this day, the Kelly Baxter disappearance remains unsolved. If you have any information that may help authorities, please contact Victoria Police.

"JULIA."

On March 1ˢᵗ 1999, National Oceanic and Atmospheric Administration (N.O.A.A.) hydrophones recorded an underwater sound so loud it was heard across the entire Equatorial Pacific Ocean array. That sound was dubbed "Julia."

The origin of the Julia sound remains unknown.

\#

Do you know how many lives the sea claims each year? How many bodies it swallows, never to be seen again? Yes, we recover some, but how many more are lost to the darkness forever? Where else but a graveyard would you find so much discarded flesh?

Is it any wonder that its depths are filled with monsters?

\#

Sounds, taken out of context, can be open to interpretation, our life experiences framing how we perceive them. You heard claws scratching at your window, I heard the branches of the oak tree in our yard. You heard a scream in the night, I heard a fox crying in the fields by our house. I still hear your cries for help.

When I first heard the *Julia* sound, I knew exactly what it was.

#

March 5th 1999

"…Richardson's already written it off. Says it just sounds like another *Upsweep* recording. But there's something different about this one. Doesn't sound like an iceberg running aground to me."

I wasn't listening. I refilled my glass. A cheap scotch blend that I'd picked up from the liquor store a block from our house. Cheap and large. The quickest possible exit from reality, please. I hadn't waited to get home before I opened it. Formalities are for people who don't really need a drink in the first place.

"Would you give it a listen if I send it to you?"

No.

"Tom? You there?"

I drained the glass and refilled it. "Send it over."

"Oh, okay, great. You've got the best ear in the acoustics business, Tom. I'll send the file straight away. Er…"

Here it comes…

"Look, Tom. I'm really sorry about what happened…"

I ended the call.

The world had been moving at a crawl ever since the accident. Time stretched taut over broken glass memories. Eventually something was going to tear. I don't know how long after the call I booted up my laptop, but Bob's email was waiting for me when I did. No subject, no message (too awkward), just a .wav file attachment.

I slipped my headphones over my ears, picked up my glass and hit *play*. The drink didn't make it to my lips. That was the first time I heard the voice.

#

March 7th

If you want to save the starving children, you can forget it. If you want to throw millions of dollars at Mars or the Mariana Trench, well, there's a billionaire for that. Add in some naming rights for whatever you discover and you'll likely have a bidding war on your hands. We raised the funds for the expedition in twelve hours. Two days after Bob sent me the email, I was the only passenger on a six-seater plane descending to land at the N.O.A.A. base at Cape Adare, Antarctica. I watched the black peninsula of the cape come into focus. A coastline of high, jagged, basalt cliffs spread across the otherwise perfect white landscape like a stain, like the inky corpse of some huge beast washed up from the ocean thousands of years ago. I couldn't think of a better place to begin the expedition.

In the two days since I'd received Bob's file, my headphones had barely left my ears. I'd listened to the recording hundreds of times. I'd filtered it to lessen the background noise, played it at different speeds to account for the ocean temperature and depth at which it was recorded. The sound had been picked up by multiple hydrophones along the N.O.A.A. array, which meant Bob had been able to triangulate it with some accuracy. His calculations suggested that it'd come from an area between The Bransfield Strait and Cape Adare. I guessed that was why Richardson had dismissed it as an iceberg grinding along the ocean floor. Had he even listened to it properly? There was no doubt it was organic.

Maybe he and Bob hadn't recognized it because they hadn't heard it before. Maybe it was because it wasn't meant for them.

#

When you spend your life on the ocean, when you love it intensely, it can be easy to forget how callous it is. How insignificant we are to it, how out of place on its surface, or in its depths. It wants nothing more than to consume us, to drown and devour us. When our yacht capsized, I was on the main deck, my wife and daughter in the cabin below. Maisie had always been scared of confined spaces, made us keep the cabin door open whenever she was below. That was how the sea got in so fast.

#

You don't just hear a scream underwater, you feel it, too. As we touched down at Cape Adare, the recording swelled against my ears. I closed my eyes and pressed my headphones tighter. I felt the sound mixing with the rush of my blood in my skull. I felt the cry in my heart.

Around me the plane juddered and skidded to a halt. When I opened my eyes again, the black cliffs towered all around me. The dark peninsula had consumed me.

#

March 8th

At its deepest point, the Bransfield Strait

measures two kilometers surface to seabed. The largest iceberg in the world reaches between six and seven hundred feet down. That's only around two hundred meters into the sea. Given, the Strait isn't all as deep as its deepest point, but what chance was there really that the sound was an iceberg scraping the sea floor?

Our crew consisted of two deep-sea acoustic technicians (Kyle Hillerman and Geoff Holt), an underwater videographer who'd been part of the '85 team who discovered the Titanic wreck (Conrad Janssen), an ROV operator (Kelly Blake-Peterson), the captain (Don Grosse) and his second, and a photographer supplied as part of our funding deal with our billionaire benefactor. Loading the ship took a whole agonizing morning, but by lunchtime on the 8th we'd set sail. *I've heard you, and I'm coming.*

#

It's hardly state-of-the-art, given the value of each of the sonobuoys, but in order to deploy them you tie a sandbag to them and hurl them into the sea. The sandbag anchor drags the hydrophone to the ocean floor; a surface float marks the spot of deployment for later retrieval. Kyle and Geoff began dropping buoys at five-mile intervals along the Strait. I sat below in the lab watching the jittering green line of the spectrum analyzer screen, listening, and waiting. Kelly monitored the live data on her own laptop. If we got a good hit from the hydrophones, she'd deploy the ROV, piloted from a console across the table from me. Windows on either side of the cabin looked out onto the freezing waters as we carved a slow path along the trench.

#

March 10th

We were an hour from sunset when Geoff called through the hatch into the cabin: "Bob, come take a look at this."

I hauled myself up the metal steps and onto the main deck. A layer of ice, sea spray turned to glass, made the upper deck treacherous. We trudged towards the bow, where Kyle was leaning, peering into the black water below.

"More here…" He pointed.

I looked over the side. A dead fish bobbed past my view. Then another followed it. I watched as five more slid along the side of the boat, bounced against the hull by the current.

"What are they?" I asked.

"Looks like rock cod." Kyle leaned further over the side.

"We've been seeing them for the past hour or so. Just one or two to begin with, then these groups of about ten." Geoff ran a hand over his beard; his glove came away covered in ice crystals.

"I wonder if there's been a chemical spill out here." Kyle was attempting to prod one of the fish with a hooked pole we used to drag buoys from the sea.

"That might explain why nothing's eating them," Geoff added.

"What do you mean?"

"Well, we've not seen a single predator, no birds circling, no seals, no larger fish. These rock cod are a free lunch and no one seems to want 'em."

"Christ!" Kyle had wandered around to the bow of the ship. He was looking out at the sea ahead of us.

"What is it?" called Geoff, but fish had already begun spilling along the sides of the ship.

"G! G!" Kyle was frantically waving to Geoff to join him. I followed.

As far as we could see, stretching out across the Strait, hundreds of silver bodies swelled on the waves, rising and falling all around us. A thousand dead eyes staring forever more into the sky. A thousand dead eyes watching the last rays of sunlight draining from the day.

"Good God."

Or perhaps they were fixed on the depths beneath us.

"Tom! Tom!" Kelly called as she scrambled up onto deck. "We've got a hit!"

#

Maisie's hand had a way of appearing in mine. We might be walking along, or sitting on the deck of the yacht, and I'd feel her little fingers reaching across my palm, waiting for my hand to close around hers. She liked to hold hands, and I liked it too. She was only five, but she was smarter than her years, and fiercely independent. She already did so much without me or my wife. It was nice to feel that she was still my little girl for a while longer.

#

I sat at Kelly's laptop, headphones pressed tight against my ears.

"Frequency's really low," Kelly noted, tapping at the spectrogram excitedly. "It's loud, too. Big."

I closed my eyes. *I'm here.* I listened.

#

I can't think of a worse way to die. When our yacht capsized, the sea flooded the boat with such ferocity that it filled the cabin in seconds. I was on deck when the whole world turned over. As the yacht rolled, it dragged me underneath it. I was sucked into the darkness, past the cabin; I slammed into the bow and was spat out into the ocean.

I lay on my back, looking up into the perfect blue sky above me. I didn't know how I'd gotten there. My mouth was full of blood. I must have hit my head when the boat went over. I could hear frantic hammering but I couldn't tell where it was coming from. I turned to ask Maisie if she could answer the door, but instead I rolled into the water and it was her face I saw screaming against the glass of one of the cabin windows below.

I'd never seen fear like that. There was madness in it: my little girl, who was afraid of confined spaces, trapped in the flooded cabin, small pockets of air above her growing smaller all the time. She thrashed and kicked at the glass, bubbles exploding from her mouth as she screamed.

I dived down until I was on the other side of the pane. I beat my fists on it until my knuckles trailed blood in the water. I managed to grab ahold of a rail above the window and swung my legs at the reinforced glass. My feet just skidded over it. Behind Maisie, I caught a glimpse of my wife, her lifeless body buffeted in the wake of Maisie's thrashing.

The door! Maisie, swim for the door!

She insisted we kept it open when she was below deck. It'd been open when the boat rolled. I hammered on the window, trying to get her attention, but she'd twisted away from the glass, pressing her face into an ever-shrinking pocket of air above her.

Please, sweetheart. Swim for the door!

I hauled myself along the upturned hull until I found the ladder into the cabin. As I did, I felt the boat shift. The bow dipped. The boat was beginning to sink.

I grabbed the handrail and launched myself up the stairs. I slammed into the closed cabin door.

NO! NO! NO!

It must have swung shut when the boat rolled. I threw myself against it, tried to force it with my shoulder. Bubbles of precious air swarmed around me, freed from the cabin, racing for the surface. There was a gap between the door and the frame! I forced my arm through, frantically swinging and snatching for whatever was holding the door closed.

My whole body screamed, screamed for air, screamed for Maisie, screamed into the darkness that was drawing over my eyes. I felt something brush against my hand, on the other side of the door. I grabbed at it and held it.

It was Maisie's hand.

I'm here, honey, I'm here.

The last air left my lungs in a sob.

I'm sorry.

I'm so sorry.

I held on tightly to her hand. It was so small, so still.

Please take me with you.

The boat was tipping, sinking fast now.

I held on for as long as I could.

#

I'm here.

"Some kind of mass mortality event…" I could hear Geoff explaining to Kelly about the fish. I pressed the headphones tighter to block him out.

I'm here.

The spectrogram danced, blue and red, streaming across Kelly's laptop screen.

"…HELP…"

It was heavily distorted, but I knew what I was listening for. In the first recording the voice had been too degraded to make out the words. I knew who it belonged to, though.

"…HELP US."

It was my wife's voice. Julia's voice.

#

The crew of a fishing boat pulled me out of the water. I should have been dead, I wanted to be dead, but the sea, in its infinite cruelty, had spat me out again.

Coastguard divers were sent to retrieve Julia and Maisie. I sat on the deck of the response boat staring at my empty hands.

After a time, the divers returned. Something was clearly wrong.

The cabin was empty. They'd found the boat resting on its side on the seabed. The cabin door had been open. Whatever had been blocking it had likely been dislodged when it grounded.

It fell upon a red-faced young man to tell me the details. He assured me they'd continue to search until Julia and Maisie were found, but two days later the search was called off.

The whole thing was ruled an awful freak accident. No one was able to explain how a boat, piloted by an experienced sailor, had come to capsize on seas as calm as they were that July day.

#

The first recording had begun with my wife's voice. Too distorted to hear clearly what she was saying, but it was unmistakably her. It had ended with Maisie's scream, the two sounds converging on the spectrogram. Wherever they were, they were together.

We'd taped a map of the Bransfield Strait to a whiteboard in the middle of the lab. Kelly stood by the map.

"The first buoy is here." She drew a circle. "The second…here." Another circle. "Because we only picked up the sound on two buoys, we can't triangulate it accurately. My best guess, from a rough analysis of the data, is that it's coming from further up the strait. Ahead of us."

"And leaving a trail of dead fish behind it," added Kyle.

"What if it's not organic?" Geoff said.

"Sure looks like it is from the data." Kelly was taping a copy of the spectrogram onto the map.

"What if we're tracking some classified Russian sub? Maybe it's leaking something that's killing all the fish in its wake."

"If it is, great. We can ask them if they've got any good vodka on board, because fuck me, I'm cold and I could use a drink." Don toasted us with his coffee mug.

#

I excused myself and headed to my cabin. Kyle and Geoff would take it in shifts to continue to drop buoys through the night. They told me they'd wake me if we got any more hits.

In my room, I began to work on cleaning up the recording. The first pass through the software was going to take six to eight hours.

Almost a year before, I'd held my daughter's hand as she drowned, watched my wife's lifeless body sink to the bottom of the ocean. Now, somehow, Julia was calling to me, sending messages that had brought me halfway across the world to find her. I couldn't allow myself to follow that thought any further. Never finding their bodies, never being able to bury or say goodbye to my family, had broken me. I knew madness, knew that it coiled inside me. I'd seen it in Maisie's eyes as she thrashed against the cabin windows. I saw it in my own eyes whenever I glimpsed my reflection.

I stood at my porthole looking out. The corpses of hundreds of fish, picked out silver in the boat's floodlights, slithered past as we ventured deeper along the strait. Death pressed against the boat on all sides.

Tell me how I can help you. Tell me what you want me to do.

#

March 11th

"Tom. Tom, wake up." Kelly knocked on my cabin door.

In my dream, Maisie was hammering on the cabin window. I started awake. The knocking followed me out of my sleep.

Kelly called again. "Tom? Are you awake?"

I'd fallen asleep watching the progress of the recording being filtered. Ten per cent left to go.

I hauled myself off my bunk and opened my cabin door. "What is it?"

"Something you need to see."

I followed Kelly through the boat. Geoff and Kyle were waiting for us in the lab. It was obvious something had spooked them.

"Why aren't we moving?" I asked.

"You'll see."

Kelly led me over to her laptop. "Just before 5am. we began picking up a new signal. Higher frequency that the last one."

"Something smaller?"

"Once every forty-eight hours, Don brings the boat to a full stop. Does an hour of checks before we head off again. It was about half an hour after he'd stopped that we started picking up the sound."

I looked at the spectrogram on the screen. "That's not organic."

"Right."

"But I was able to triangulate it. Because it was picked up on the last ten buoys we've dropped. At the same time."

"That's not possible."

"Just tell him, for fuck's sake," Kyle growled.

"Follow me."

Kelly led me up onto the main deck. The cold was startling.

"Look." She pointed over the side. I recognized the marker straight away, an orange ball bobbing on the surface. One of our sonobuoys was sitting about twenty feet off the starboard side of the boat.

Then her hand began to sweep to her right. Another orange ball bounced on the black water. She continued right.

Another marker, and then another. "They're all around us. The last ten hydrophones we dropped in the strait," she said. "The sound we picked up, it was us. We were recording us."

"Who's watching who here, huh?" Geoff said grimly.

#

It took most of the morning to haul all of the sonobuoys back in. Kyle tried to suggest that maybe they'd gotten tangled, that we'd been dragging them as we'd been deploying them, but none of them were twisted together.

Geoff suggested sending Conrad or the ROV down to see if there were any signs of how the buoys had come to be circling us, but Don wouldn't have it. "We've lost enough time to this. Funding's only paying for a ten-day expedition. Losing a morning can soon turn into losing a day if we don't get moving."

He was right. I left Kyle and Geoff resetting the equipment and headed back to my cabin. Don followed me to my door.

"Can I talk to you?" He let himself inside.

As soon as I was through the door, he closed it. For a long moment he stood looking at me, as if he was sizing me up, deciding whether or not to tell me what had brought him to my room. I noticed that my laptop had finished processing the recording from the night before. I turned it to face the wall, away from Don's view. It wasn't meant for him.

"What's going on, Don?"

"I didn't stop the boat this morning. I just told your crew that," he said.

"What do you mean?"

"'Bout four thirty, I went to get coffee. Left Chuck at the helm. He's young, but he's a good second." Don shuffled, foot to foot, a surprisingly childish movement for such a large and usually self-assured man.

"Okay."

"I'd just made it to the galley when everything went off. The whole place just, snap, into darkness. Then I felt it."

Don looked at his feet again, only this time he was reliving what had happened.

"I thought, *shit, Chuck's gone and grounded us, run us onto an iceberg*. I could feel the grinding coming up through the hull, through my feet, into my legs. I dropped my mug and I ran." Don was talking faster now, his voice shaky. "Only when I get to the helm, there's no ice. Just the black water of the strait all around us. And Chuck. Poor kid's confused and scared half out of his mind. Says that just before the bow spotlights went out, he saw something in the water. Said it was just under the surface. A huge shape. Said it stretched across the channel as far as he could see. He thought it was rising, thought it was gonna hit us. That's when the grinding started."

"Did you see it?"

"No. I felt it, though. Something scraping along the hull. I went up onto the top deck, and that's when I saw those buoys circling the boat. 'Bout ten minutes more and all the power came back on again. I've been running checks all morning, and there's no reason it should have been off in the first place."

"Where's Chuck now?"

"I gave him a stiff drink and sent him to his bunk to try and get some rest."

"You think he was mistaken?"

"Do you? What is it you're looking for, Tom? What do you think's out here?" Don's tone had changed. His fear had backed him into a corner. Now it was turning into something else.

"I don't know."

"You don't know, or you don't want to tell us?"

"I don't know."

"I trust Chuck. If he says he saw something, he saw it. Better hope, for all our sakes, that it was just a whale. If I think we're in danger, I'll turn this boat around, do you understand?"

You won't do that, Don.

#

I went straight from closing my door on Don

to the laptop on my bunk. The recording had finished processing. Filtering the audio had revealed a peak of sound after the first two pulses (HELP US). A third band on a slightly different frequency: a different voice. Like the first recording, this one contained two voices. Maisie spoke after Julia. A single word: RISE.

> HELP
>
> US
>
> RISE.

I dragged my cursor along the recording. I listened to Maisie's voice again. I closed my eyes and tried to picture my little girl. I hadn't heard her speak for almost a year. I hadn't thought I'd ever hear her again.

"I miss you," I said. My throat closed on the words. Tears streaked my face.

Even with my headphones on, I heard the screaming from above me.

#

I scrambled up the steel steps and out onto the main deck. It was Kelly who was screaming. Chuck was dragging her backwards, towards the bow, by her hair. One of his hands gripped a clump of her hair; he jerked and pulled at it as he dragged her. The other held what looked like a large shard of glass, pressed tight against her throat.

Despite the near freezing temperature, Chuck was only wearing a pair of shorts. His bare feet skidded over the slick boards, leaving a trail of bloody footprints as he staggered backwards.

Most of the blood was his. His bare chest and legs were covered in jagged gouges. A flap of skin hung loose from his abdomen, peeled away to reveal the raw muscle beneath. I was struck with the awful thought that he'd tried to flay himself.

Geoff edged up the deck after them, shaking hands held up in front of him to urge calm.

"For Christ's sake, don't fight him, Kel," he pleaded.

I passed Don, standing with a hand clamped over his mouth, utterly paralyzed by what he was seeing. Chuck slipped and Geoff let out a small cry. He just managed to keep his balance, but blood had begun to run down Kelly's jacket where he'd nicked her.

"Chuck!" I called. "Chuck, let her go!"

"I SAW IT!" he screamed. "I SAW THEM!"

"Please," Kelly whimpered.

"What did you see, Chuck? What was it, Chuck?"

"There are hundreds of them. They're bringing it to the surface, raising it up."

Off the port side of the boat, the sea had begun to bubble, to churn. Could it hear us?

"Who are, Chuck?"

Geoff shot me a horrified look. I knew what he was thinking, but I had to know.

"*Who*, Chuck?"

"You know! You brought us here! You know!"

Chuck had dragged Kelly to the bow. They had nowhere left to go. Chuck pressed against the railings, his feet slipping over the deck as if he hadn't realized he'd reached the edge. He kept stepping, kept leaning backwards.

"Chuck! Please, stop!" Geoff pleaded.

Chuck stopped. He turned to look straight at me. Then, with one terrible movement, he jerked Kelly's head back, raised the shard of glass high, and drove it down into her right eye socket. A jet of fluid and blood squirted into the air, it rained down over Chuck and the deck. At the same moment the sea lashed at the side of the boat, as if the water had risen to meet the gore. Chuck scissored down Kelly's cheek with the shard. He drove it in with such force that I heard it snap in the wound. Kelly clawed at Chuck's arm, at her face, flailing and screaming. He yanked what remained of the shard from her cheek—Don was crying out behind me, "NO, GOD NO!"—grabbed her hair once more and threw her over the side.

Geoff had collapsed onto his knees. He was crying into his hands.

Chuck rocked against the railing. He raised his head up, exposing his neck to the sea. Then he scored the shard across his throat, opening it up, spraying blood into the ocean. He collapsed forward, following Kelly into the hungry waters below.

I ran to the bow, skidding over the bloody boards. My hands grabbed at the railing to stop myself from following Kelly and Chuck over the side. The sea below was frothing, red foam splashing over the hull. I thought I saw an arm gliding just beneath the surface.

I grabbed one of the hooked poles used to drag in buoy markers, and jabbed it into the water. A pair of hands rose out of the red waves and wrapped around the pole. I felt their pull immediately, I was barely able to hold on. They were too small to be Kelly's hands. When I realized who they belonged to, I dropped the pole.

"Maisie!"

I tried to reach the pole, snatch it back, but it sank beneath the surface. I leaned over the rail, hooking my boots against the uprights so I could lean further out.

"Maisie! NO! MAISIE!" The pole disappeared below the waves.

As I watched, the whole sea seemed to darken. A huge shape was passing under the boat. It rose until I could see grey, mottled skin. It rose until I felt it grinding along the bottom of the boat. Then it opened its eyes.

As far as I could see, the ocean turned to look at me. Hundreds of milky orbs, watching me from below the crimson foam, seeing me, seeing everything. I could feel their gaze inside my skull, as sure as jagged fingers burrowing into the darkness that grief had spawned there. They searched out my pain, my anger, and feasted upon it. All the time, a huge noise, static I couldn't decipher, swelled through me, louder and louder. I clamped my hands over my ears to try and block the sound out, to keep my mind from shaking apart.

I lurched against the rail, the creature's ancient eyes pulling me forward. My feet slipped free. Kyle grabbed my shirt and hauled me back onto the deck. I lay on the blood-streaked boards and screamed.

#

The shard that Chuck used to murder Kelly had come from the mirror in his cabin. The rest of it had been reduced to a bloody mosaic in the sink below. This was where he'd cut himself.

"Christ," groaned Don. He looked like he might pass out at any moment. "Why the hell would he…? I mean I've known him for years…since he was a kid."

"Sit down, Don."

He slumped onto Chuck's bed and rested his head in his hands.

After Kyle had thrown me onto the deck, and I'd lost sight of the creature's eyes, the static had faded from my mind. It hadn't gone altogether though. I could still feel it in my ears, a constant vibration, a hum. The thing was still nearby.

Chuck had sliced patches of his skin from his body, discarding his flesh onto the floor around the sink.

"We have to turn back," Don spoke into his hands.

"No." I'd seen Maisie with my own eyes. There was no way I was turning around now.

"What? We've got no choice! You saw what happened. We can't carry on!"

"No. We're closer to the open sea than we are to Cape Adare. We go on. You want a rescue? That's the way we go," I lied.

Don got to his feet, fast.

"No! You don't want us to get rescued." He closed the distance between us, spat the words at me. "Chuck said it! You know what's out there. You know what caused this, what made him do…"

His eyes were full of tears.

"This is my boat. I'm the captain, and I'm turning it around."

"No, you're not, Don." I reached into the sink. I felt the glass slicing into my fingers as my hand tightened around it. I raised a shard and slashed it across Don's throat.

I missed with my first strike, jamming the shard into his windpipe. Don stumbled backward, gasping, air whistling out from the wound with a sickening, hissing moan. He threw up a hand to try and deflect my second slash but he was too slow and I connected with a vein. He tried to grip, tried to cover the gash, grasp for the blood that was spouting from his neck. I slashed again and again, the static roaring in my ears. The hum had risen to a scream. The creature had returned to feed once more. I slashed until Don's legs buckled and he fell onto his backside on the floor. He sat for a moment, as his life pumped through his fingers and poured down his chest. He opened and closed his mouth, trying to scream, but air just bubbled and gurgled out of his ruined neck.

I knelt down, my legs close to giving out too. "I'm sorry, Don. I can't turn back now." I dropped the broken mirror piece.

Don rocked over, crumpling onto his side. Moments later he was dead.

#

When Kelly and Chuck had fallen over the bow, when the beast had brought Maisie up from the crimson sea, a huge spike of sound had been caught on the sonobuoys. It'd spiked again when I'd attacked Don.

I listened to the recording in my cabin. It was a single word, repeated over and over by my daughter and my wife: MORE.

I knew what I had to do.

MORE.

If you could see your family again, the family you thought you'd lost forever, is there anything you wouldn't sacrifice?

Is there *anyone* you wouldn't sacrifice?

#

March 16th

Maisie's hand had a way of appearing in mine. It did again this morning.

I lay on my bunk, eyes closed, the hum buzzing in my ears, whispering a promise almost fulfilled. I'd woken from a dream of us holidaying on our yacht. I could hear Julia in the galley, singing while she prepared lunch. In the dream, I sat on the main deck looking out at the ocean. A perfectly calm cerulean sea, with a cloudless sky above. I could feel the sun's warmth on my face. A small hand slipped into mine. I closed my fingers around it.

Held it tight.

Held on.

Please don't go again.

The hand followed me out of my dream.

I didn't dare open my eyes for fear that Maisie wouldn't be there. I felt the hand tugging, urging me to get up. It was time.

#

After Don, I killed the photographer. I lured him up onto the main deck, jumped him, and choked him out with his camera strap. I then threw him into the ocean with sandbags tied to his legs. Each time another member of the crew died, the creature rose higher and Julia and Maisie called to me more clearly.

MORE.

Conrad was next. I smashed his skull with an oxygen tank and then tipped him over the bow. After I was done, I found a trail of small, wet footprints leading along the deck. They ended at the railing where Maisie had returned to the sea. With each death my family drew closer.

I knocked out Geoff and Kyle with a large dose of sedative from our medical supplies, emptied into their water rations. I tied Geoff's hands above his head and used rigging rope to drag him along behind the boat as I navigated the strait. I heard him screaming as the beast rose to consume him.

A new recording was waiting for me when I descended into the lab.

SOON, Julia promised.

SOON, Maisie echoed.

That just left Kyle.

\#

Maisie tugged at my hand, pulling me out of bed. I kept my eyes closed as she led me through the ship and up onto the deck. I could hear Kyle struggling against his bindings, pleading through the gag I'd fastened over his mouth.

"Open your eyes, Daddy."

"But…"

"It's okay, Daddy."

I opened my eyes.

She was gone. Kyle was lying, bound, at my feet. Like Geoff, his hands had been tied above his head. I didn't remember doing that. The rope from his arms stretched to the winch used to lower the ROV. His legs had been tied to the ROV itself. Had Julia done this?

Kyle thrashed against his bindings.

We'd left the strait in the early hours of the morning, and were heading further into the open ocean. I'd spotted a burning boat in the distance the night before. I wondered if a loved one's call had led them here. More boats had gathered overnight. More grieving souls? More blood for the beast?

MORE.

I released the ROV and watched as it began to lower towards the water. Kyle's ropes snapped taut. He was lifted off of the deck as the ROV dropped into the sea. The deeper it descended, the tighter his bindings became. He wailed through his gag; his body was stretched until there was the awful sound of limbs popping from their sockets. Moments later, his skin began to tear. Kyle came apart with a wet rip. His lower body sank with the ROV, his organs uncoiling into the ocean behind it.

I wandered up to the bow to wait.

I could see more boats in the distance now, and ahead the water had begun to bubble and churn. It was rising.

Soon a thousand eyes would breach the surface.

Soon Julia and my Maisie would return.

I sat on the deck and looked down at my bloodstained, empty hands.

"TRICK."

I was sure it was going to go wrong. It was going to go so very wrong.

Johnny was the runner. He was fast. Much faster than me. As soon as the door opened he was off. I'd barely got the "Help!" out of my mouth before he'd barged past her and into the house.

That year we'd dressed as Michael Myers. Yes, both of us, as Michael Myers. You see, we both really wanted to be Michael Myers and neither of us was gonna give up on that plan. So, in the end we called a truce and two Mikes it was.

That had caused Russ Glick to point in Johnny's face and yell: "Stoopid! There can't be two Michael Myers!"

I'd explained to him—because I'd given it quite a bit of thought—that it made sense. If there were two Mikes, that'd explain how he could be off in the distance and then "BANG!" right there to kill ya! Russ chewed it over...then had to admit it made sense. Shortly after that, two Mike Myers kicked Russ's ass and stole all his candy.

Now the shoe was on the other foot and it was Mike Myers who was terrified. I was terrified.

I was 10, Johnny just 8. We'd decided early on to go further afield, head out to the edge of town. To the spots where no one tricked or treated. We thought the good spoils would be out there. We hadn't expected anything like this.

"It's Celia!" I tried to explain. "She was trick an' treating with us. But she ran off! We think she might have run into a yard or someone's house!"

The woman. It turned out her name was Cassie. Was in her 30's. In fact, she was 33, if I remember rightly. I'm sure that's what the paper said. To begin with she'd been confused, then angry, then her expression had softened as I'd explained.

Johnny had shoved past her, almost knocking her off her feet. He'd hit the foot of the stairs and run. He had a set of those trainers with the lights in the heels. It was like someone had let off a strobe in the dimly lit hallway as he'd hammered upstairs.

Cassie looked over her shoulder.

"Well, she's not in here!" she protested.

I continued to apologize, while trying to look past Cassie and take in as much of the ground floor as I could. A room to the left: looked like the lounge. I'd check there first. Kitchen: at the end of the hall. A door under the stairs; could be a cellar.

Cassie turned to head after Johnny. He wouldn't be done yet! I grabbed her arm and pleaded again for her help. Could she see right through me?

Cassie put a hand on my shoulder. "It's OK. We'll check the yard. Just…wait here. OK? Wait here."

I watched Cassie head up the stairs. Hopefully I had bought Johnny enough time.

As soon as she was gone, I hurried into the lounge.

Empty.

Cassie clearly liked candles. The whole house seemed to be lit up with them. I checked around the room. Everything seemed to have a motto embroidered or printed on it. *Love Every Moment! Seize The Day! I* seized a bunch of ornaments off a shelf by the door, sweeping them into the plastic pumpkin I'd half filled with treats. I shook the pumpkin till the ornaments disappeared, sinking beneath a sea of candy.

I could hear Cassie pleading with Johnny upstairs. "We'll look for Celia. She's not up here! Come downstairs with me." Just a little longer Johnny!

Next, I checked the kitchen. No one there. Some loose change on the counter: swept into the pumpkin. I found a pair of scissors in the cutlery rack by the sink. I grabbed them and shoved them in my jumpsuit. My hands were shaking. I was sweating. I don't reckon my heart could have beat any faster. I thought I might puke.

Just the cellar left. I hurried across the hallway to the door under the stairs. I stopped with my hand on the handle. I tried to turn it quietly. The latch was stiff. I shook it and it flipped up.

I realized I could no longer hear sounds above me. I froze. Then Cassie and Johnny were on the stairs and heading my way. I quickly stuck my head around the door to the cellar. Darkness. Later I'd laugh at myself for that.

Cassie and Johnny hit the bottom step. I raced through the kitchen to the back door. "Can we check out here? Please?" I called, cupping my hands against the black glass pane that looked out into the yard.

Johnny joined me at my side. "No one upstairs," he whispered.

"Same down here." My breath fogged on the cold glass.

Cassie joined us. She flicked a switch by the back door, and the yard was flooded with white light. "Where did you last see her? Your sister. She was trick or treating with you?"

"She was there one minute and then… I just figured she'd gone to the next house ahead of us. But when we got there, they said they hadn't seen her."

The back yard was empty. A gate headed into an alley that ran back to the main street. I'd pocketed the back door key. I apologized for Johnny again and we thanked Cassie for letting us check her house. I saw a group of trick-or-treaters passing the end of the alley. "Celia!" I called to them. "Celia! That's her!" I pointed and we ran off after the group.

Of course, none of them knew us.

"Celia? Who's called Celia nowadays?" laughed Johnny.

"Shut up!" I punched him in the arm. "It was the best I could come up with at the time. Did you get much?" I shook my plastic pumpkin to show Johnny what I'd got.

"Wow! No way!"

Parked across the road from Cassie's house was an old Ford pick-up. Dark green with a layer of darker green along the side where the panel had been replaced. Johnny and I approached it. The guy inside wound down the window.

"How did we do?"

"Fifty dollars each? That's what we agreed, right?" I wasn't going to get ripped off.

"Yeah, yeah." He pulled out two $50 bills and held them just back from the window so I couldn't grab them.

"Any chance of a bonus?"

"Depends. What ya got for me?"

I handed him the back door key. "There's no one else home. We checked all the rooms."

The guy in the truck started to laugh. He pulled out another couple of $20s and handed the lot to us. "Happy Halloween, kids."

We'd headed to the edge of town because we thought the good spoils might be out there. We hadn't expected anything like this. Michael Myers and Michael Myers stuffed the notes into their boiler suits and headed to the house next to Cassie's to carry on trick-or-treating.

"THE SCREAM."

The end began with a single scream.

We watched the man stumble between a group of Japanese tourists. The woman recording reeled back with a yelp when she saw him. She swung her cell up to his face, catching the horrified expressions of her friends behind him as she did.

Someone yelled, "Daijōbu desu ka?"

The sun flared on the screen of Alex's iPhone. I leaned closer, blocking out the glare with my shadow. A message from Sandy popped up on the screen: "Where r u?"

The man in the video moaned. His hands were clamped over his face, white fingers gripping at the flesh as if he was trying to hold his skull together. He dropped onto his knees. The cell camera followed him down.

His groaning began to change. The muscles in his neck were spasming, taut cords twitching and straining. Something snapped, a loud pop that sent the woman recording scuttling back. In her panic she recorded the floor, the feet of other commuters gathered to see what was happening. The groaning became an awful wail.

"Dear God."

"Sandy sent it to me." Alex didn't look up. "It's Edison Central. The police have closed it off, she said."

When the woman's camera found the man again, his hands had slipped from his face. His mouth had stretched so far open that it looked like the twitching muscles in his throat might dislocate his jaw. His head jerked back, pulling his gaping mouth even wider. It jerked again, and I had to look away. The man's agonized scream seemed endless.

"*Christ*. Turn it off." I couldn't watch anymore.

"They're saying it might be a terror attack. Gas or something released inside the station."

"Gas doesn't target just one person." Bob's voice made me start. I hadn't realized he'd been standing behind me.

"What, then?" Alex scrolled the video back with his finger.

"Turn it off. I don't want the kids seeing that." I looked across the park to Sarah and Georgia, sat on a picnic table deep in conversation. Georgia perched on the tabletop swinging her legs over the side, while Sarah knelt on the bench beneath her.

Since Sarah turned eight, she'd grown less interested in parks for any of their rides, and more interested in finding a quiet spot, generally as far away from me as possible, to talk with Georgia and sip the latest Starbuck's frappe variation. They swapped tall drinks, sipped each other's, laughed and then swapped back. I was grateful that they hadn't heard the video.

"Now?" Behind me, Alex sighed into his cell. "Yes, okay. I understand. Sandy, we're five miles from Edison Central. Even if it was a gas attack…"

Bob joined me watching the girls. "You okay?"

I nodded. I wasn't.

"I miss the days when we only heard about terrible things, didn't have to see every single one of them."

"I miss those days too, Dad."

Alex paced as he talked. "Yes, yes, I remember the July London attacks. I know there was more than one bomb, but Sandy, they haven't even…"

After 9/11, we'd all tried to get back to normal, but what we'd known as normal before that September day was gone for good. Normal now was waiting. Waiting for the next bomb, the next mass shooting, the next virus. 9/11 had long, skeletal fingers that could easily reach through twenty years to wrap themselves around your heart. In 2015, Tom and I had Sarah. That same year, he was diagnosed with cancer. It was inoperable. We waited for the chemo to work. It didn't. We waited for a space on a clinical trial. It never came. We waited until he died in January of the next year. Normal now was waiting.

"No, no, I don't think you're being unreasonable. We'll see you soon. Sandy, it's okay." Alex hung up his cell. I was already heading across the park to collect Sarah.

*

On the ride home, Sarah pouted and prodded about our reasons for leaving early. I deflected as best I could, my mind replaying that video over and over: the man's ever-widening jaw, that awful wailing. As we'd climbed into the car to leave, I could have sworn I heard a scream in the distance.

*

"Mom, what the hell?"

A car had swerved across the road ahead of us. Its front end had collided with the median barrier. I stopped a way back. There wasn't any smoke, any shattered glass, no skid marks on the road. The driver hadn't been going very fast when they crashed.

"I'll go and make sure everyone's okay." I opened my door and made to step out. Sarah called me back.

"What if it's a carjacking, Mom?"

"I don't think they're gonna want to swap that car for ours, kiddo," Bob said.

I looked back to the car. I wasn't sure what brand it was—a Lexus, a Tesla, maybe—but I knew it was expensive. Still, between Sarah's caution and the knot I had in my gut from Alex's video, I dragged my heels as I approached the crash.

"Hello? Is everyone okay?" I called.

No answer. Damn it.

I arrived at the driver's side window. A woman sat facing away from the glass.

"Hello? Are you hurt?" Still nothing.

I assumed she was talking to the car's passenger; I could hear muffled sounds coming from inside the car. I leaned closer, reaching out to tap on the pane.

"Hello?"

As I did, I caught sight of the car's passenger: a man, I guessed in his sixties, his cheeks glazed with tears, an expression of utter horror contorting his face. He'd pressed himself back as far as the cabin would allow. He was frantically running his hand over the door behind him, trying to find the handle but unable to tear his gaze away from what he was seeing.

"He…he…hel…"

He found the catch and he ripped it back, throwing the door open. He fell out of the car, dropping momentarily out of sight. Now I could hear his muffled voice clearly.

"...P! HELP! OH, GOD, HELP!"

I heard one of the doors of our car open. Afraid it was Sarah, I turned to look back. At the same moment, the woman in the car in front of me threw her head backwards. She spasmed back with such force that her head slammed into the glass, leaving a splatter of blood and hair on the pane. She began to wail. She gripped her head with her hands, fingers tangled in her gray hair.

Her head jerked back again, this time crushing her fingers against the window. More blood smeared on the glass. I stumbled away, almost losing my balance as I turned to run.

The sound of the door had been Bob climbing out to see what was happening. His confused expression quickly turned to alarm when he saw my face.

"Get back in the car! Get in the car!"

As I ran, the woman's awful wailing grew louder behind me. It felt so close that I expected to turn and see her racing after me.

I was back in the car before Bob.

"What's going on? What happened?" His questions were lost in my panic. Behind us, another driver honked. Cars had begun to back up on the road.

I started our car and peeled forward, mounting the sidewalk to get around the Lexus. Even then we scored along its trunk as we passed.

"Shit! Mom!"

"Please don't look, Sarah."

All the time, the woman slammed her head against her window, only now her gray hair was black, slick with dark blood.

*

I don't know how many times Bob asked me what happened before I found the words to answer him. He was scared, obviously, and not doing a great job of hiding it in front of Sarah. She just sat silently watching me from the back seat. I was sure she'd seen the woman we'd fled from. As we drove away, the passenger (*her husband*?) ran around their car. He'd waved his arms madly, trying to flag down some help. The car that followed us had almost hit him in their panic to get past.

"It was the same as the video."

"Christ." Suddenly our car felt very small, too tight for all the awful thoughts squirming through my mind. I wound down my window.

Bob turned back. "You think they were at Edison Central too?"

I drove. Maybe the woman in the car was having some kind of seizure. Maybe it wasn't related to the video at all. Maybe she needed my help and all I'd done was run away. I stopped about a mile down the road, got out and called 911. I instinctively walked far enough away from the car that I thought Sarah wouldn't be able to hear. When I got through to someone, I told them about the accident, gave them the address. I hung up when they asked for my name.

*

Thirty excruciating minutes later, we pulled into our street. Along the way, I'd noticed several cars pulled haphazardly off on the side of the road. I tried to convince myself they were simply breakdowns, the usual abandoned cars you see at the side of the freeway, coincidences I was interpreting as something else, but I was sure I'd seen at least one figure crouched beside one of those cars.

A woman was kneeling in the middle of the road.

I slowed to a crawl as we approached. Her body was arched so far backwards that she shouldn't have been able to support herself; still, somehow, she knelt screaming silently into the sky. Her mouth was stretched open, even further than the man in the video. Her eyes were unblinking, staring behind her, watching us as we approached.

"Turn around, Kate." Bob's voice was barely a whisper.

"Our house is on the other side of her." I had no plan other than getting us home. I wasn't going to fail Sarah in that.

The car jolted as we rode up onto the curb. Sarah let out a yelp. Aside from that, we were all silent. I was holding my breath.

I'd chosen to pass the woman with her on my side; that way, she'd be as far away from Sarah as I could manage. She passed alongside the car's hood. I continued on until she was almost level with my window. That's when I heard it.

Faint at first. The sound of strained rasping, air wheezing from her impossibly gaping mouth. The woman was still breathing. No, she was still screaming. Only her body had contorted so unnaturally, her muscles pulled so taut, that she could only manage to snatch the thinnest of breaths to cry out with.

I wound up my window against the terrible sound.

As we passed the woman, I couldn't help but look into her tortured eyes. They didn't move or acknowledge us. Could she even see me anymore? I was having trouble breathing. I gripped the wheel, trying to keep myself together. It was so terrible, so unthinkable. In one of the buildings close by, someone wailed.

I panicked. All the fear that'd built as we passed the twisted woman poured out. I sped forward, almost slamming us head-on into a telephone pole on the sidewalk. I took Bob's wing mirror off as I swerved to avoid the post.

I stood on the brake and the car skidded sideways back out into the road. We jerked to a stop that made my seatbelt lock.

"Fuck. Fuck. Are you okay? Sarah? Dad?"

I put my hand on Bob's arm.

"I'm…okay," he said, although I wasn't convinced.

"I'm so sorry, Dad."

Behind me Sarah's seat belt unbuckled. I spun to see what was happening. She was up on her knees looking out the back window.

The wailing was out on the street behind us now.

"Sarah, get back in your seat."

"Mom! Mom!" She waved frantically out the back windshield. "That's Jenny Derby."

"Sarah, honey, please sit back down. We have to go."

Jenny was Sarah's age. She'd lived on the same street as us since Sarah was a few months old. Framed in the back window, Jenny stumbled towards the car. This couldn't be happening.

"What? Mom, we can't just leave her."

"We have to go. *Now,*" Bob urged.

Jenny didn't make it to our car. She buckled to her knees in the road. Her hands were clamped around her bottom jaw, her fingers hooked into her mouth. I guessed she was trying to force her mouth to close.

Maybe her fingers were locked, contracting like the cords in her neck, but when her head jerked backward she didn't—maybe she couldn't—let go. Her mouth gaped, wider, wider, her head pulling so violently against her locked hands that her lower jaw dislocated. It came out of its socket with an awful crack.

Jenny's wailing was unbearable. Her bottom jaw hung useless, gripped in her hands.

I took off before we could witness what happened next.

*

We drove without speaking. Sarah sobbed against the back seat. Bob stared out of the window at the passing countryside. After what happened to Jenny, I'd torn out of our street, driven in a blind panic, too fast, without direction, unable to pull a single thought out of the red haze that descended over my mind. I had no plan, no idea what we could do next. When I saw the sign for Mount Callaghan, I took the exit.

Before Sarah was born, Tom and I spent a lot

of weekends hiking the trails at Mount Callaghan. We'd camped there, too. Sarah didn't know, but she'd been conceived there. We hadn't planned to stay on the mountain that night, but our car broke down. We were carefree enough back then that we'd embraced the whole thing as an adventure, had a dinner of trail bars and bananas, and slept across the back seat of our car. Nine months later, Sarah was born. I desperately wanted to comfort her now, but that would mean stopping, and until I knew what to do next, I couldn't stop.

"It's going to be okay, honey," I said, even though I knew they were just empty words. I had no idea what was happening, what awful thing would happen next, if I could even protect us from any of it.

The incline was growing steeper, narrower, the canopy of the trees lining the sides of the road met overhead. Sunlight strobed over the car's hood. I drove the ascent to Mount Callaghan.

One of my fondest memories of our camping trips was of the silence of the place. It was so peaceful. Tom and I would often hike a whole day without seeing another person. It was that memory of a vast emptiness that guided my hand to take the road we were driving. Whatever was happening, I hoped that being away from other people would help me keep Sarah and Bob safe a while longer.

Bob turned from the window.

"That poor, poor child." His voice was a hoarse whisper. He thumbed tears from his eyes.

"I know." I put my hand on his arm. I called Bob *Dad*, but he wasn't my father. He was Tom's. We'd been close since we first met, not long after Tom and I began dating. My father died when I was a teenager, and Bob had easily fit into a space that'd long been empty in my life.

About eighteen months after Tom's death, I got a call at three o'clock in the morning. It was Bob. He'd taken a pretty nasty fall down the stairs at his place. He managed to drag himself along the hallway to the phone and called me. I asked him if he'd called an ambulance. He repeated that he'd called *me*.

Later that night, as we sat in the ambulance that *I* called, I asked him what he was doing up at three in the morning anyway. The painkillers must have kicked in because I don't think he'd have told me otherwise. He said he fell at eleven on his way to bed, but it'd taken that long for him to accept that he wasn't going to be able to pull himself up the stairs to his bedroom and that he needed help. That was when he'd hauled himself along the corridor and called me.

I wheeled him out of the hospital two days later. All the way home, he argued that he was perfectly capable of looking after himself. That he could roll the *damn wheelchair* on his own. Not that he needed it, of course. I told him that was fine. If he was so healthy, he could look after Sarah and me until the plaster came off his broken leg. I drove him to our house and he ended up staying with us for almost a year.

I had no problem with that at all, and Sarah loved having him live with us. She hadn't had a chance to get to know her father, and Bob was always ready with a tall tale about Tom's adventures growing up. He always finished with "and that's how I got this gray hair," pointing to a different one each time. I'd known and loved Tom for more than ten years, but Bob always seemed to have a new story about him that I hadn't heard before. I missed Tom terribly, and sitting listening to Bob talk, well, it felt like it brought him closer somehow.

The road was getting steep. Bob leaned across and switched on the radio. He scanned the channels until he found a news report. The newsreader didn't seem to know much more than we did. They speculated that a number of terrorist attacks had occurred across the city. That a nerve gas might have been released. They cut to a reporter at Edison Central. At that point, the line seemed to go dead. The host cited technical difficulties, called the reporter's name a few times—only the line wasn't dead, it wasn't completely silent. There was a faint whistling of air, the same wheezing I'd heard as we passed the twisted woman in our street. At the other end of the line, someone was trying to scream.

"Dad, please turn it off."

Bob didn't move.

"Dad, please."

I turned to see Bob, staring straight ahead, his arms locked across his chest, hands gripping at his sides.

"Are you okay?"

The road doglegged ahead of us. I swung around the curve and almost into a truck that was parked side-on, blocking the way forward. Two figures, dressed in head-to-toe protective gear, appeared from the woodland at the side of the road.

"Road's closed. You can't go this way," one of the figures called.

"They've got guns, Mom," Sarah whispered from the back seat.

The figure talking to us had a handgun, held down at his side.

"Turn around," called the second man.

"Government quarantine," the guy with the handgun added.

I noticed movement in my rear-view mirror, another figure stepping out from the woodland behind us. This figure was dressed differently: their protective gear consisted of the kind of N-95 mask we'd all worn during the pandemic, and they wore hunting camo, with a rifle slung over their shoulder.

I cracked my window open. As I did, I noticed one of the men in front step back away from us. "We live up here. We're just heading home," I lied.

"Close your window, ma'am."

"Road's closed," a voice barked from beside the car. The masked hunter had drawn up alongside us. More alarmingly, they'd drawn the rifle from their shoulder.

"Mom…"

"I said, we live up here. We're just heading home. Let us through, please."

"Close your window and back the fuck up," growled the hunter.

I kept the window open; it seemed to be keeping the men at a distance for now.

"Head to my house." Bob struggled to get the words out through clenched teeth.

"Dad, are you okay?"

"Grandpa?" Sarah leaned between our seats.

"Sit back, honey…please."

In front of the car, *Handgun* was pacing. He gestured to the hunter next to us. I didn't like the way he was waving his gun around.

Bob opened his door.

"Dad, no." I grabbed at his arm. The muscles spasmed beneath his shirt. I only held on harder. "Oh no, Dad, no."

"Just get to my house. Keep Sarah safe…" Dad wrestled his arm from my grip. He staggered out onto the road.

"GET BACK IN THE FUCKING CAR!" The hunter had his rifle up, pointed at Dad.

"NO! PLEASE!" I begged.

Dad began to wail. Ahead of us, Handgun opened fire.

I slammed my foot on the accelerator and raced forward. I only meant to put the car between Dad and the gunfire, but I rammed into Handgun head on. We slammed into the truck barricade, crushing him between the two vehicles. His cries were awful.

Handgun's accomplice didn't stop to help him. He turned and raced away into the woods.

I fumbled the shifter into reverse. I had to get back to Dad! A gunshot rang out behind us.

"NO!"

In the rearview mirror, I saw the hunter stumble backwards. Even though the shot had done a terrible amount of damage to Dad's head, he still wailed into the sky. The hunter raised his rifle again.

I stood on the accelerator.

My tires squealed over the asphalt. The hunter's second shot exploded as we collided with him. He crumpled under the trunk. The car jerked upward and then dropped as we rolled over him.

I didn't stop.

We kept speeding backwards.

My foot was jammed to the floor. My heart was going to explode. I screamed in anger, screamed with the unbearable grief of it all, screamed because there was nothing else I could do.

The back end of the car swung across the road.

I couldn't stop.

I wasn't in control anymore.

We ran up the verge, into the woodland, and slammed into a tree.

*

The back windshield had shattered. A branch stuck through it like an arm reaching in to take hold. Sarah had fallen into the footwell behind mine and Dad's seats. She wasn't moving. I tried to reach for her, but a bolt of pain shooting across my chest made me snatch my hand back.

"Sarah?"

I unclasped my belt and threw open my door. I tried to step out but my legs gave way underneath me and I collapsed onto the dirt.

I crawled to the back passenger door and hauled myself up. When I saw the bullet hole in the window, something inside me snapped. As I'd reversed at the hunter, I'd heard his gun discharge, a huge noise close by the car. No! No! I was just trying to protect Dad. I hadn't stopped to think what might happen if we put ourselves between the hunter and his target.

I ripped the door open.

Sarah groaned.

"Mom?"

"Sarah? Oh, honey, I'm here." I climbed onto the back seat and, even though the pain knifing across my chest was excruciating, I pulled Sarah up next to me and clung on to her.

"Are you okay? Are you hurt?"

"I just fell. Is Grandpa okay?"

"No, sweetheart, no, he isn't"

"Why is this happening, Mom?" Sarah started to sob. She buried her head against my side. I held her with all the strength I had left in me. We cried together until the sun no longer flickered in the canopy above us, and the woods around us had swallowed the last of the day.

Exhausted by her grief, Sarah finally fell asleep against me. I gently laid her across the seat and ventured outside.

The evening was quiet, the woods around us that'd concealed Handgun and the others were unnervingly still.

The hunter lay where we'd hit him. As I approached his body I wished for a sound to distract me, for any other sound than the one I heard coming from Dad. The hunter's first bullet had removed most of Dad's head. Even in the near dark, I could make out the glistening wreck of his skull. Jagged edges and bone where his face should have been. He should have been dead, surely he *was* dead, but still he knelt, the remains of his head arched up into the sky, air whistling out of his lungs. Even in death he screamed.

I picked up the hunter's rifle. I wanted to cover Dad, but I didn't have it in me to get any closer to him. I fumbled through the pockets of the hunter's vest and found some extra rounds. When I'd finished, my fingers were streaked with his blood.

I buckled Sarah into the back seat, laid the rifle where Dad had sat, and started our car. I managed to rock us back and forth until the car dislodged from the tree and rolled back onto the road. Between crashing head-on into the barricade truck and reversing into a tree, the car was in bad shape. I had no idea how far it would carry us. I hoped it would get us to Dad's place. His house was another ten miles past Mount Callaghan. The land it sat on had once been used to rear cattle. It was a large house without any neighbors for miles around. It seemed like a good place to stop, to take stock, to hide if need be.

As I drove past Dad's corpse, I prayed that his screams would fall silent soon. He'd saved us. I prayed that I might live long enough to save Sarah, too.

"THE GOREY MAN."

<u>1.</u>

The women watched their children weaving between the trees at the edge of the wood, circling the cracked-bark trunks of the oaks as they were stalked.

A shriek was followed by laughter.

"Tig! You're it!"

The game began again.

Constance watched her boy, watched him disappear from view where the canopy closed above and the light of the warm spring day no longer touched the ground. She watched him from the field they called Woods Entrance. No adult was permitted to enter the woods.

Constance watched her boy and her friend, Isemay, watched her.

"How many years have we been doing this?" Isemay asked.

"Three. Willem will be four before the harvest."

"Then that'll be three years of me watching you worry," Isemay joked. "My friend, your time will come."

"We only have one more year. Willem will be too old after that."

The older children in the village had another name for Woods Entrance. They called it "The Gorey Man's Field." They spoke in whispers of a beast, made somehow of bone and branch, with the head of a dead animal, an elk—some said a goat or a wolf— rotting atop its shoulders. A beast that called the woods its own: the Gorey Man.

Those children said its belly was a cage of twisted tree limbs, twined branches that held the bodies of the children it fed upon, corpses it carried with it, the young swallowed forever into its awful frame.

Constance got to her feet.

"Come on," she urged. "Come on." She looked off, along the tree line, at the other mothers watching the woods and waiting. Every mother from the village with a boy of age was there.

A call went up, further along Woods Entrance. Everyone turned to the voice.

"A child has been taken!"

Costance looked back to Isemay.

The voice called once more, "A child has been taken! The King of the Harvest has chosen!"

Someone cheered, "The crop is safe!" Another whooped in celebration. The mother of the boy was raised onto the shoulders of a crowd that had gathered around her. They chanted and danced and paraded her along the tree line.

"The King has chosen! The King has chosen!" they cheered.

Other mothers called their children back from the woods. Some hurried to the edge and waved to their boys to come quickly. None of them stepped into the King's domain.

Children began to emerge all along the wood's edge.

Isemay's son, David, joined her at her side. Constance watched Willem play. She didn't call, didn't approach the trees.

"There's always next year," Isemay consoled her.

After a time, Willem bounded from between the trees and hurried back to Constance. She picked him up and hugged him.

They followed the celebratory procession back to the village.

2.

By the time they marched back into the village the air was already heavy with the pine scent of burning juniper. As they passed the village gates, Elders waving bundles of branches wafted smoke over the procession. The smoke made Constance's eyes sting and Willem cough.

While the women had been away at Woods Entrance, the men of the village had been preparing the spring feast. Spits had been erected in the village square, and lambs were being roasted for the evening's celebration. The daughters of the village had gathered spring flowers and woven them into garlands that they hung around the necks of the returning mothers. Others sprayed the women with droplets of blessed water collected from the sacred river that wound through the King's woods.

As they turned to approach the village square, Isemay noticed her friend's pace slow. She smiled warmly and held out a hand to beckon Constance to continue with her, but Constance was already slipping from the group.

"Don't be disappointed, my friend," Isemay called to her.

Still carrying Willem, Constance turned her back on the procession and took her boy home.

<u>3.</u>

That evening the men and women of the village danced in lines around the huge bonfires erected in the village square. They drank honeyed mead and feasted on roasted lamb and veal. They cast the bones into the fire, where the remains sizzled, and the fat popped and bubbled.

"Drink and dance! The King of the Harvest will be watching! Give thanks to him!" called the Elders.

The fires cast flames so high they could be seen from the Gorey Man's field.

"Give thanks to him!"

*

Constance listened to the cheering as she packed. She'd shuttered the windows on her single room home, tried to close out the noise of the festival. Willem dozed on a sheepskin. He'd fallen asleep early, exhausted from the hours of play at the wood's edge.

Constance wrapped some salted meat in cloth. She packed the cooked eggs that she and Willem had painted to celebrate the arrival of spring, along with some bread. In a corner of the room, she moved aside a small cabinet and began to dig in the dirt where it had sat. At first, she scraped at the soil. Then she began to gently part the earth as she drew closer to her prize. She found the hilt and eased the blade from the ground.

It had belonged to Willem's father. The village women weren't allowed to own weapons, so she'd hidden it after his death. She wiped it on her dress. It was old, the blade blunted by time and use, but it would do.

Willem stirred and rolled over in his sleep. She turned to her sleeping son,

"You are good enough," she said.

By the time the cock crowed, Woods Entrance would be filled with drowsy workers ready to plow the field for sowing. She needed to be gone before they arrived.

<u>4.</u>

Willem followed behind Constance as they slipped from the village in the darkness before morning.

"Don't dally, boy," she chided him.

By the time they reached Woods Entrance, Constance was carrying him.

A few of the men from the village had fallen asleep on the bare earth. Constance put a finger on her lips to warn Willem to be silent. She stepped carefully across the dark field, straining to see the way ahead of her. She couldn't carry a lantern for fear of being seen as she left the village and so she made her way slowly, placing each foot down cautiously until she neared the edge of the woods.

"We will follow the river," she told Willem. "Every thing needs water to live. If we follow the water, we will find the King eventually."

Long ago, the Elders had decreed that no adult may enter the woods. No man or woman should cross the threshold at Woods Entrance and trespass on the King's sacred land. With Willem in her arms, Constance disappeared between the trees.

<u>5.</u>

Although the sun had risen beyond the wood, under the thick canopy of the trees it grew no brighter than first light. Constance and her boy trudged through the thick undergrowth, over downed branches, she lifted him over fallen logs and slippery, moss-covered rocks.

Constance had heard stories of wolves and other feral animals stalking the forest. At Evening Worship, the Elders would recite cautionary tales of villagers who'd stumbled into the wood only to become a meal for a pack of salivating wild dogs. She kept her blade ready, listening for any sounds around them, but, aside from their own footfalls, the wood was eerily quiet.

The deeper they travelled, the more alike each yard of silent thicket became. When at mid-morning they stopped to eat a light meal of the bread and meat that Constance had packed, it was as much an attempt to get her bearings as it was to sate her and Willem's hunger.

They continued on, but with each mile they walked, Constance grew less certain of their direction. She had expected to find tracks, signs that the King stalked the same woods they trudged through, but all she had seen was endless, dizzying green.

Finally, she threw up her hand. "Listen!" she hissed. It was the whisper of water, the distant murmuring of the King's river. At last! She closed her eyes, relief flowing through her.

"We follow the water. We'll find what we came for," she told her boy.

Constance carried Willem towards the sound of the river. Her son had done well, walked for most of the morning without complaining, but he had begun to flag and she knew that they likely had plenty of ground to cover yet. He was strong but slight, and she would be able to carry him on her shoulders for several miles before she needed to rest.

Ahead, the trees thinned, and the air around Constance cooled until her arms prickled. As she neared the edge of the wood, more sunlight flared in the canopy above her, but it didn't bring with it the warmth it promised.

"Close your eyes, boy," she instructed Willem. As the trees grew fewer, her view of the riverbank ahead grew clearer, and with it, the bodies that lay there.

<u>6.</u>

Constance stood over the elk. The body of it, at least. The head was nowhere to be seen. The wound was a mess. No hunter from Gorey had done this. No hunter from Gorey would've left all this prime meat behind. She wondered if a bear had attacked the animal while it drank from the river.

That might've made sense if it wasn't for the other bodies scattered around her.

She passed a second elk, rabbits, foxes, each with their heads taken, lying on the bank. The kills were fresh, the meat not yet spoiled. Their blood had turned the earth to mud.

Constance steadied herself as she stepped through the gore and continued along the river. What kind of an animal would kill so indiscriminately? If it had sprung upon the first elk, the other animals would have fled. If it had dragged its kills to the riverbank, why was there so much blood where she now walked? And why were so many of the kills dead in the same position, with their legs tucked beneath them, as if they'd dropped to their knees to die?

Constance had reached the blessed river, and she intended to continue along it until they found what she'd come for. She felt certain of one thing: they were headed in the right direction.

123.

*

Constance had heard of them, but she'd never seen one with her own eyes: a tree bent so far over that its trunk formed an arch. The oak curled above her. Willem stretched out his hand and traced his fingers over the rough bark.

The oak's crown had grown into a claw that swayed and scratched at the earth beside them. If it continued to dig downwards, eventually it would bury itself. As they passed beneath the oak, she was able to see more bent trees ahead; they were entering a tunnel formed from the twisted trunks.

Two thoughts entered her mind at once. They arrived with such clarity that it was as if another voice had spoken them to her. *This is the entrance* was one of them. The other: *Do even the trees bow before the King of the Harvest?*

7.

As they'd walked, the sound of the river rushing alongside them had grown softer, more faint, until it only whispered of freedom beyond the tunnel of trees. As they'd walked the trees had bent lower. At first, it'd been enough to lift Willem from her shoulders, but now she was leaning forward herself, ducking beneath each arch. Soon she would need to crawl to continue on.

Then, without warning, the ground fell away ahead of her. Startled, Constance lost her footing and fell onto her back. She tumbled down the bank, landing hard on the root-covered ground beneath. Thick, twined tree roots snaked across the dirt around her. She was at the base of a huge tree.

"Be careful, boy!" she called up to Willem, who stood at the edge of the drop. He sat down, hanging his legs over the side, before pushing off and sliding down the bank, cheering as he skidded.

Constance climbed to her feet. She picked up her blade and inspected the way forward. At the foot of the tree, where the roots should have met the ground, there was only darkness. A tunnel had been hollowed out of the dirt, something had dug beneath the tree. The entrance was large enough for her to crawl through. That made it far too large to be the burrow of any forest animal she knew.

Constance leaned close to the darkness. The air beyond was thick, warm, and she felt it move over her like an exhaled breath. With that breath came the stench.

For the first time since she'd entered the wood, Constance considered fleeing. A bright red flare of panic set her heart slamming. She smelled the ripe stink of a carcass left for the flies, of a sick animal's pen. Of blood and feces.

Constance turned from the tunnel. She swallowed hard on the half-digested food rising in her throat. She gripped her blade until she felt the hilt digging into her palm. She waited for the nausea to pass. She didn't run. She wouldn't run. Instead, she knelt and opened her bag. She took out her tinderbox and the small lamp she'd packed.

At the bottom of the bank, beneath the cover of the bent trees, where the air was still, it was easy for Constance to light the char in her tinderbox. As the sound of her striking the flint onto her fire-steel echoed in the still forest around her, she was reminded of how eerily quiet the place was, as if she and Willem were the only living things for miles around.

She melted some of the wax from the lantern's candle onto the smoking char and soon had a small flame she could use to light the wick. She gently returned the lit candle to the lantern.

In the jittering light of the lantern, Constance looked up to see Willem watching her, his eyes fixed ahead.

"What is it, boy?" she asked.

It took a moment for her to realize Willem was looking past her to the tunnel entrance. She turned with the lantern to the dark opening behind her.

The lantern's light had pressed the darkness back into the throat of the tunnel. All along the wall of the passage were deep grooves, as if something larger than the tunnel itself had forced its way through. Constance edged closer to the darkness; it retreated before her lantern's glow. She peered into the shaft ahead. More grooves were scored into the walls and the floor. In the tight space, her lantern would suffice to light the tunnel around them as they walked. If the light were extinguished, though, they'd be lost in the crowding dark. She returned to her satchel one more time and retrieved a ball of flax twine. She fastened one end to a thick tree root that hooked out of the ground. She gave the ball to Willem.

"Unravel the twine as we walk," she instructed him.

Constance turned back to the darkness. She ducked beneath the loose roots that trailed from the roof of the tunnel. The thick, wiry fibers reminded her of the tails of rats. She felt them tangle in her hair, scratching at her scalp. The feeling made her skin crawl, but she would not turn back.

She held her blade in one hand, the lantern in the other.

"Stay behind me, boy," she cautioned Willem as they entered the King's lair.

*

There were lengths of the tunnel where Constance could stand upright, and there were sections where she had to stoop to pass. She wondered how the King navigated the passageways. Constance wasn't tall by any means, and she'd imagined the King would tower over her. If that were the case, why weren't the tunnel ceilings higher?

As they walked, Constance stepped around the grooves that had been carved into the dirt at her feet. They resembled the ruts made by carts, although no cart would fit into these tunnels. No cart would leave tracks in the walls and the roof either. So what had created them?

"Watch your step, boy," Constance warned Willem, who silently unraveled the flax twine behind her.

Constance had no idea how far the tunnel would stretch, how deep it would wind beneath the woods. What was very clear, though, was that ahead the tunnel was pitch. Behind them, darkness caught at their heels. They were a single, feeble light moving through otherwise shapeless, smothering black.

The deeper they trod, the stronger the rancid stench grew. Constance stopped. She turned back to Willem. He squinted at the lantern light. She knelt in front of him and reached into her bag. She retrieved a small cloth pouch filled with dried petals and herbs.

"Here, hold this over your nose when you need it. The scent will help with the smell."

As they ventured further into the lair of the King, more and more questions had spiraled in Constance's mind. What kind of animal lives among its own waste and the rotting carcasses of its prey? What kind of animal could have scored the deep furrows in the walls around them? What kind of animal was the King of the Harvest?

Of course, she'd heard the stories of The Gorey Man, but those stories were for campfires and teenage children.

She knew the truth from those who'd seen the King themselves. She'd heard it from the mouths of the Elders. She knew that the King of the Harvest was a mighty protector, that it guaranteed the harvest and their survival. That all it asked for in return was a single worthy child on the first day of spring.

Ahead, Constance heard quiet sobbing, the exhausted crying of a child.

"We are almost there, boy," she spoke in a hushed voice.

As they trod, the tunnel began to open up around them. No longer did Constance need to duck to pass. They had arrived at a large chamber.

The sobbing sound was coming from the wall of the chamber. In a small alcove, more akin to a grave in the village barrow, was the boy who'd been taken the day before. Across the opening of the grave, thick roots twisted over one another. It was impossible that they'd grown there in such a short time, but they held fast when Constance tried to move them.

"Hush," she whispered to the boy. "Is the King here?'

The boy nodded. Constance turned and slowly swept the light of her lantern across the chamber. In the middle of the space, branches had been piled, heaped upon one another. The way they'd been stacked and twined together reminded Constance of a nest.

She lingered on the odd construction. The lifeless eyes of an elk drew her attention to the floor by the nest. Constance turned her lantern to the carcass, expecting to highlight the remains of a deer. Instead, she found that the elk's neck ended in a rough wound. The beast's decapitated head had been impaled on a large branch. Behind it, her lantern's light reflected in another set of eyes.

A wolf, its head also impaled, watched her with glassy eyes.

Constance returned to the trapped boy. She raised her blade and began to slash at the roots that blocked him in.

To her horror, the roots shifted of their own accord, slithering away from her strikes. They scuttled backwards, up the dirt wall. Constance followed their retreat with the light of her lantern.

Their movement reminded her of a spider, or maybe fingers feeling over the chamber's dirt as they searched for a handhold.

They found it in the wall near the chamber's roof, hooking into the dirt like a claw. Trailing from the roots, a branch-like limb stretched back to the nest.

Another claw skittered over the roof. This one was different, though. The fingers of the claw were bones. They looked like ribs to Constance. The bones burrowed into the dirt above her. Hanging from them, a second branch arm, cords of root fibers swelling and tightening around it as it straightened and lifted the King from its nest.

Constance looked upon the beast with a horror she had never before experienced. The stories had been true: the King of the Harvest was a monster, a thing of branch and bone, somehow animated when it should not have been alive.

Constance grabbed at the boy in the wall and hauled him from his prison. He fell to the dirt at her feet.

The King of the Harvest continued to unfurl. More claws buried their bone talons into the dirt of the chamber's walls. More leverage to pull the King up.

Then the elk head stirred. It rose into the air, lifted by the branch it was impaled upon. Another head rose beside it; the wolf, then a bear skull, and more still, ascended until The King of the Harvest was surrounded by the decapitated heads of its prey.

Some were fresh kills, possibly from the riverbank last evening, others were older, their flesh bare of fur, their meat slick with decay. They moved together, tilting and following Constance's movements. She knew that was impossible, that death had long since stolen their sight, but still she felt their cold gaze upon her.

The King of the Harvest rose to its full height. As it did, Constance felt a weight fall upon her shoulders. She felt herself being pushed down. Unseen hands tried to bend her, to force her to kneel before the King, but she would not so easily buckle.

She took her blade, and she drove it into a thick tangle of roots at her feet. She felt the pressure on her shoulders falter. Constance pulled the blade from the ground and then drove it down once more. For a moment she was able to stand fully again.

In that moment, she looked to the many heads of the King, and she roared, "Listen to me! My boy is good enough. You hear me? My boy is good enough for you!"

*

The sun was low, and the workers were packing their tools to return to Gorey when the figure appeared at the edge of the trees at Woods Entrance. The woman held a blade that reflected the setting sun in bands on the trunks of the oaks around her. Although she was slight, she seemed to radiate a strange power that made the men in the field reluctant to approach her. A child stepped from the trees and joined her at her side.

Constance looked down at the boy. "Go home now," she instructed him.

She did not know the boy's name. Nor had she recognized his mother when she'd been raised onto the shoulders of the other villagers the day before. She had no interest in him or his kin.

Constance watched the boy race across the freshly plowed earth of Woods Entrance. Soon the crop would be seeded. It would grow and it would be plentiful all because of her Willem.

She'd known it each time she'd taken him to the Spring Offering at Woods Entrance, and now she'd been proven right.

"You were good enough, my boy. You were good enough," she said softly, and a proud smile spread across her face. Constance stepped from the trees and began the walk back home.

ANDREW CULL

Andrew Cull is an award-winning writer and horror director. He's the author of *Bones, Remains,* and, most recently, *The Cockroach King.* He's also the co-editor of the FOUND series of found footage horror anthologies. His story collection *Bones* has been described as "a masterclass in emotional cinematic horror fiction."

His new novella, *She Says Die,* is coming at you with teeth bared and a loaded shotgun in 2025.

Andrew lives in Melbourne, Australia. He loves horror and Hitchcock, and, like you, he's not easily scared.

Follow Andy on Bluesky: @andrewcull.bsky.social and Instagram: @andrew_cull.

Also by Andrew Cull:

REMAINS

Grief is a black house.

How far would you go? What horrors would you endure if it meant you might see the son you thought you'd lost forever?

Driven to a breakdown by the brutal murder of her young son, Lucy Campbell had locked herself away, fallen deep inside herself, become a ghost haunting room 23b of the William Tuke Psychiatric Hospital.

There she'd remained, until the whispering pulled her back, until she found herself once more sitting in her car, calling to the son she had lost, staring into the black panes of the now abandoned house where Alex had died.

Tonight, someone is watching her back.

Aurealis Award Nominee for Best Horror Novel (2019)

Also by Andrew Cull:

BONES

Four Stories. Four Monsters.

BONES brings together four chilling ghost stories by award winning writer-director Andrew Cull. Four monsters collected in paperback for the first time.

DID YOU FORGET ABOUT ME?
HOPE AND WALKER
THE TRADE
KNOCK AND YOU WILL SEE ME

"A masterclass in emotional cinematic horror fiction."
—Kendall Reviews

Australasian Shadows Award Nominee for Best Collection (2018)

FOUND

An Anthology of Found Footage Horror Stories.

Between April and August 2021, eighteen horror writers disappeared. Gathered together for the first time, these are the stories they were writing at the time of their disappearances.

Stories by: Holly Rae Garcia, Jeremy Hepler, Bev Vincent, Ally Wilkes, Clay McLeod Chapman, Nick Kolakowski, Tim McGregor, Alan Baxter, Angela Sylvaine, Josh Rountree, Georgia Cook, Ali Seay, Donna Lynch, Kurt Fawver, Robert Levy, Joe Butler, Fred Fischer IV, Aristo Couvaras.

Reader caution is advised. Readers of this anthology have reported nausea, feelings of anxiety, paranoia and hallucinations after reading the texts included.